Calling Maggie May

Calling Maggie May

Anonymous

Simon Pulse

New York London Toronto Sydney New Delhi

〰 SIMON PULSE

An imprint of Simon & Schuster Children's Publishing Division

1230 Avenue of the Americas, New York, New York 10020

This Simon Pulse edition June 2015

Text copyright © 2015 by Simon & Schuster, Inc.

Cover photograph copyright © 2015 by Getty Images/Take A Pix Media

All rights reserved, including the right of reproduction in whole or in part in any form.

SIMON PULSE and colophon are registered trademarks of Simon & Schuster, Inc.

For information about special discounts for bulk purchases, please contact

Simon & Schuster Special Sales at 1-866-506-1949 or business@simonandschuster.com.

The Simon & Schuster Speakers Bureau can bring authors to your live event. For more

information or to book an event contact the Simon & Schuster Speakers Bureau at

1-866-248-3049 or visit our website at www.simonspeakers.com.

Designed by Karina Granda

The text of this book was set in Adobe Caslon Pro.

Manufactured in the United States of America

10 9 8 7 6 5 4 3 2 1

Library of Congress Control Number 2015936199

ISBN 978-1-4814-3902-2 (hc)

ISBN 978-1-4814-3901-5 (pbk)

ISBN 978-1-4814-3903-9 (eBook)

Calling Maggie May

Wed, Sept 17

Swim meet: First place in the freestyle today! And second in backstroke.

Calculus test: 97%

Tues, Sept 23

Swim meet: First place in backstroke, third place overall.

American History: 80% on quiz

Wed, Oct 1

Chemistry: 92% on test, A on lab report

Math team: Fourth place in meet. (No prizes for fourth place, Mom notes.)

Fri, Oct 3

English: A- on essay

Swim meet: Third place in backstroke, second place in freestyle, didn't place overall.

American History: B on paper

I deserved an A, but Mr. Franklin hates me. Now I'm screwed.

Why do I even bother? I'm only keeping this journal because Mom is making me. Guess she's going for the Tiger Mom of the Year Award. "You're a junior now. You have to keep track of all your accomplishments so you'll have things to write on your college applications!" Right. Like colleges really want to read this litany of mediocrity. What's the point of noting all my near misses for the admissions committees? "It worked for Mark!" she singsongs in Chinese, smiling encouragingly.

I'm not Mark! Do you hear that, Mom? Mark had straight As all through high school. Mark lettered in three sports. Mark was editor of the newspaper. Mark won every debate, every Science Olympiad, every math team meet, every EVERYTHING. I get it, okay? Everyone gets it. Mark certainly does. . . . I can see the pity for me in his eyes every time he comes home from college. His poor, stupid sister, who can't do anything right.

The only person who doesn't get it is Mom, who still believes I have it in me to be a genius. Who still thinks I can get into Stanford, if only I really apply myself. Mom is living in an FOB fantasy.

Jenny Hsu taught me that the other day: FOB for Fresh off the Boat. Not that my parents are fresh anything. . . . They emigrated from Taiwan more than twenty years ago, before Mark and I were even born. But you'd never know it to talk to them. They still speak Chinese at home, and Mom switches into English only for words or phrases she has learned since coming here. A lot of these have to do with college applications.

Dad isn't as bad. He works as a hospital administrator, so he speaks English all day, but with an accent that makes me cringe. I think I'd actually rather listen to him speak Chinese, even though I understand only, like, 70 percent of what they say. Maybe it's better that way. It's all nagging anyway.

Sometimes I think Dad just wants me to be happy, but Mom would probably spit on that phrase. So American, she would say (in Chinese). Coddling kids, telling them anything they do is fine. How are they going to be happy if they are not successful?

She has a point, I guess. It's a tough world out there, and if you don't stay on top of it, you could be chewed up and spit out.

I know she just wants the best for me. She worries that I am too Americanized because my Chinese is crap (not like Mark's!) and I watch too much TV and my grades aren't perfect. But nothing is ever good enough for her. Well, that's not true. Mark is. But see above: I am not Mark.

She would be so pissed if she knew I was just spewing random crap about my life in my special college-prep journal. But it feels good to get it out. I'll just tear out this page later.

Mon, Oct 6

French: 96% on quiz

Swim meet: First place in backstroke, second place in

freestyle and butterfly, though that was a fluke. Second place overall.

Chemistry: 95% on test

Good day.

Thurs, Oct 9

Debate tournament: Fifth place

Newspaper: Got passed over for events editor even though I've been a reporter for four semesters and Chris has only done it for two. Totally unfair, but he's friends with the editor in chief. Of course.

Math team: Let's not even talk about it

How demoralizing. The thing is, I might do better at all this stuff if I actually cared about any of it. I'm only doing it for college. Well, I'm doing it for Mom, and she's the one who cares about college. Not that I don't care. It just all seems really . . . abstract to me. Does it really matter where I go to college? I'm not so sure it does. It just seems like a lot of money and a lot of debt, and I'm not sure what I'm supposed to get out of it.

But I keep showing up for all these stupid activities because Mom says it's important, and I'm a dutiful daughter. The only one I really like is swimming. I love swimming, which is probably why I'm better at it than any of the other stuff. Not that I'm that great. . . . I'm not even the best person on my team, let alone in the whole Seattle area. Definitely not good enough to attract serious interest from colleges.

But that's never bothered me.

I don't know, the other kids on my team all try so hard and work so hard. I work, but I don't seem to have that competitive drive. That Mark had. That I'm supposed to have. I don't care about winning or being the best or beating my best times. What I really like about swimming is the water.

That sounds dumb, doesn't it? But everything is better under there. I don't have to deal with other people—how they see me, what they want from me or whatever. When I'm underwater, I'm not a daughter or a student or a competitor. I'm just a body.

And when I lift my head to breathe, I hear the roar of the crowd and the echoing sounds of squealing kids, but it all feels far away, and a second later I'm down in that blue world again where everything is muted and wobbly. And I know it's only temporary, but sometimes it's the blue world that feels real and the dry world with all its noise and air and demands that feels like an uncomfortable dream.

American History: C+ on paper

Mom is going to kill me. Not even kidding. She'll . . . I don't even know. This is untested water. I've never gotten a C before. And obviously Mark never did. I bet Mom doesn't even know grades go this low.

I can't tell her. I'll just tell her it was an A. No, if I tell her it's an A, she'll be so proud she'll want to see it. God. Okay. I'll tell her it was a B+. She'll be mad, but she won't freak out. I'll just have to make sure I bring my grade up by the end of the semester. If I start getting As from now on, I can bring it up, and she never has to know.

I don't like hiding things, but what choice do I have? I guess I'll tear out this page later too, in case she goes snooping.

I don't know how to keep doing this. I've got so much bottled up inside, and one day it's going to blow up and destroy everything in my path like a tornado. I have to get it out, or I'll go crazy. And I have nowhere else to put my thoughts. Maybe if I had anyone to talk to . . .

I guess there are Jenny and Eiko and John and the others at the geek table, but I can't really talk to them. In the end, they're just like Mom. They might as well be spies for her. All they ever talk about is how they did on this or that test, or how nervous they are about the stupid Academic Decathlon. And if I told them I just got a C on something, they would judge me so hard. I can just imagine their faces. Jenny would be pitying: "Don't worry. You can totally bring it up if you work hard! Maybe you can ask for an extra-credit assignment!" All while calculating how much closer to valedictorian she is now. Eiko would furrow her brow, look concerned, and be like, "What's gotten into you? You used to be smart." And John would laugh at me and say I've let myself get distracted . . . and he wouldn't have to say anything more. Everyone at the table would crack up because they would all know what he meant. That I'm boy crazy. Just because Eiko told everyone that I have a crush on Tyler Adams.

I don't have a crush on Tyler Adams. . . .

I do have a small, and slightly unhealthy, obsession with Tyler Adams.

Who could blame me? Tyler's on the swim team, but he's not like me. He's amazing. I mean he actually wins things. That's not why I like him, though.

I know the reasons girls are supposed to like boys. I know that I'm supposed to love him from afar because he is intelligent, or kind, or generous, funny, and ambitious. But the truth is, I don't like him for those things. I don't even know if any of those things are true about him because I barely know him and have never spoken to him. What I do know is that he is intensely, painfully beautiful. That is something I know very, very well, because it is very difficult not to notice when you see him every day in a teeny-tiny racing suit.

So sue me. Tyler Adams is gorgeous, and there's nothing wrong with me for noticing—*not* that he would ever notice me. I am not gorgeous. I am a nerd. I am a geek. I am not cool or pretty or sexy or popular. I'm wallpaper. I'm worse than wallpaper, because people might notice an interesting wallpaper pattern. I'm beige, industrial-grade, institutional wall paint. The kind you never notice at all, unless it's to remark how totally boring it is.

Tyler would never talk to me. And besides, Mom would freak if she knew I was even looking at a white boy. John is right. I should stay focused on my schoolwork, since that's all I'm good for. Then maybe one day I'll be a huge success with my own biotech company, and then cute boys will date me. Will they? Does that work? Do cute boys want to date girls who can buy and sell them? Maybe not. Maybe I'll just buy and sell the cute boys, then.

Except I'm no good at schoolwork, either. So I really have nothing. Sixteen years old and already useless.

Wow. Colleges are going to be really impressed when I send them this. Better rip out more pages. Not yet, though . . . It makes me feel a little better to read over these rants, so I'll leave them a bit longer.

Mon, Oct 13

Calculus: 90% on test

French: 88% on test

Math team meet: Second place

And in far more interesting news, Tyler Adams almost kind of looked at me today! Wow, I am so pathetic. But it was the greatest thing that has happened to me since . . . since Dad took me and Mark to the amusement park for my fourteenth birthday? God, that was a long time ago. My life is sad.

But back to my miniscule triumph! It was on the bus home from swim practice today. I heard Tyler ask a friend of his when their next English paper was due. His friend had no idea, so Tyler stood up and called out to the whole bus, "Is anyone in my English class?" And, well . . . I am. I doubt he even knows that, since I'm sure he has never noticed me in class. But anyway, no one else said anything for a minute, and I saw my chance. I said, "Um . . . the paper is due next Thursday."

I was sitting three or four seats away from him, and there were people in between us, so he heard me but I don't think he knew exactly who had spoken. In any case, he sort of looked around in my general direction for a minute and said, "Thanks," and then went back to talking to his friend.

My brush with fame! Well, not fame but . . . attractive

boyness. Okay, writing that out, it seems so incredibly sad, it makes me ashamed of myself, but it was genuinely exciting at the time. I was proud of myself for having the guts to talk to him . . . even if he couldn't tell it was me.

Tues, Oct 14

I saw Tyler talking to a girl today. I don't even know her name, but I hate her from the very depths of my being.

That's a little crazy, isn't it? I can't explain it, but when I saw them together, all this emotion swelled up inside of me. I've seen Tyler talk to girls before—he talks to and flirts with girls all the time. He's even dated girls on the swim team, but the thought of them doesn't twist my insides the way the girl today did.

Something about the way he looked at her . . . It was different from the way he is with other girls. Somehow I knew right away: That's what I want. I don't care about college or the new debate topics or how I place in next week's swim meet. My only ambition is to be looked at like that.

What is it about this girl? I wish I knew. There's nothing special about her. As far as I could see, she's nothing but a pretty, dumb white girl, interchangeable with all the others at our school. So what was it that made him look at her like that? What does she have that the other girls don't? And how do I get it?

Thurs, Oct 16

Chemistry: 82% on test

Debate meet: Fourth place PF, no place LD.

English: 85% quiz

I was wrong about that girl. Ada Culver. The one Tyler was talking to.

I just assumed she was one of the popular girls, the ones who all blend together, with their honey-blond hair and their honey-tan skin and their skinny tan jeans. But she's not like that.

She's not exactly popular, for one thing. She eats lunch alone every day, and I never see her talk to anyone. That makes her sound like a loser, doesn't it? Like she's an even more hopeless case than I am. But that's not quite right either.

There's something sort of mysterious about her. I tried to cyberstalk her, but she's got almost nothing online. Usually the popular girls and the wannabes are all over the Internet, where they can control and curate their image from the safety of their bedroom. On the Internet, it's easy enough to make yourself look cool in front of the whole world, but her profile is totally locked down. Almost like she's hiding something.

I wonder if that's what Tyler likes: a little mystery. Or maybe it's just that she's beautiful . . . sheets of coppery blond hair and long legs like a model. I guess it's not so hard to understand the appeal there.

Thurs, Oct 23

I think I'm becoming a little fixated on Ada Culver.

Maybe it's not the sanest hobby, but it's something to do, something to think about other than the endless stream of tests and papers and competitions. I feel like if I just study her closely enough, learn everything I can about her, I could unlock her mystery.

There's something so different about her. Strange? Weird? A little off? But not in a bad way. I almost can't believe now that I ever mixed her up with the other girls at school. She doesn't dress like the popular girls. She doesn't dress like anyone else, really. It's like she doesn't even care about things like fashion and trends.

I guess people might say that about me, too (if they bothered to say anything at all about me). I don't seem to care about fashion because all I wear are baggy jeans and bulky sweaters and plain T-shirts. Definitely not the height of fashion.

But I don't think anyone could ever think Ada Culver and I have anything in common. If I avoid fashion, it's mostly because I don't have the time, don't have the energy, definitely don't have the money, and don't see the point in it. The result is that I look frumpy and invisible at all times. Whereas with Ada . . . it's not exactly that she's outside of popular style. It's more like she's above it.

Obviously money is not an issue for her, because even I can tell that her outfits don't come cheap. And it's not that she doesn't care or put in the effort, because she always looks amazing. Like, even the popular rich kids at school mostly just wear skinny jeans and tank tops or band T-shirts or whatever. They look cool, but they all look pretty much the same. But Ada . . . She dresses like a . . . like an adult, kind of? Or like a movie star. Maybe that's it.

Just an example: Almost everyone in school has these puffy ski jackets that are popular right now. And the people who can't afford those, or don't care enough to buy them, we have lumpy hand-me-downs or jackets from thrift shops that don't fit right. But Ada came to school yesterday in a perfectly fitted coat that swirls around whenever she turns, a deep blue scarf threaded with gold, and leather boots that *click-clack* on the pavement when she goes outside to smoke. No one else wears heels to school—not even the teachers.

The other weird thing is that even though she doesn't seem to have any friends at school, she's on her phone all the time. (A superfancy top-of-the-line phone, obviously, in a shiny pink case.) I always see her at lunch or between classes, looking like a model in a fashion magazine spread as she lounges against some wall and talks or texts on her phone. But who could she be talking to? And who picks her up after school? She's never on the bus. The other day I saw her get into the passenger side of a really nice car that I think was a Jaguar. I'm pretty sure no one at school drives a car like that. It must be her parents, and they must be loaded.

Okay, maybe I am being a little creepy. It's not like I spy on her. . . . I'm just curious, because she is so weird. I mean, interesting. And so different from me.

Fri, Oct 24

I did something crazy today. I wore a scarf. Blue paisley. Silk. My dad gave it to Mom for her birthday a few years back, but she's never worn it. When I was putting away laundry yesterday, I happened to see it, and before I even thought about what I was doing, I grabbed it. And I wore a dress today, too—my piano-recital dress. It's not particularly elegant or flattering. Actually, it kind of makes me look like a dumpling. But I had to do something.

This all probably doesn't sound that crazy, but for me, it is. The geek table noticed right away. They asked if I had a recital that afternoon and gave me a strange look when I said I didn't. But a strange look is better than no look at all, right? I'm not sure, but it seemed like it might be worth a try, anyway.

I don't know what I'm doing. I've been feeling a little nuts ever since I wrote that last entry. It's like expressing all those thoughts awoke something strange in me. And I know I should be worrying about my upcoming history test, and I am trying to study, but somehow all my mind wants to think about is what I can do to make myself less me and more . . . someone else. More Ada.

That's hopeless, I know, but school stuff feels hopeless too these days. If I'm not going to be the brilliant scientist Mom dreams of, maybe I can be cool and exciting at least. Enough so Tyler might know my name. I'd be happy with that.

I don't know why he doesn't just forget about her. She obviously has bigger things going on than him, though I can't figure out what. Who is she always talking to on her phone?

Wed, Oct 29

French: 84% on test

Math team: Meet, but I didn't place.

I haven't seen Ada and Tyler together in a while. Did they break up? Did he dump her? Did she dump him? A while ago I wouldn't have believed it was even possible to say no to someone as gorgeous as Tyler Adams, but I guess if anyone is in a position to turn him down, it's Ada Culver. She's probably dating someone even better now.

But who could be better than Tyler? It would have to be someone pretty amazing.

A celebrity. A prince. An alien. Or maybe no one at all. Maybe a girl like Ada Culver is so cool she doesn't even need boys.

Thurs, Oct 30

I spoke to Ada today. And to Tyler. It was so weird! I almost can't believe it really happened. Nothing this interesting has happened to me in . . . well, maybe my whole life. How can that be? How can a conversation with a couple of kids at school be the most exciting thing that ever happened to me? But Tyler is Tyler, and Ada's not just any girl, as I've already made pretty clear.

I want to get it all down now while it's still fresh in my head. I'm afraid if I go to sleep I'll wake up convinced it was all a dream. Even now I'm not so sure.

It was lunchtime. I was in line to collect my uninspiring rations of institutional-grade chicken fingers, stressing about this huge history test I bombed that morning, when I noticed Tyler moving across the lunchroom. I let my eyes follow him because even though it's painful to look at Tyler and see how gorgeous he is and think about how hopeless it is to be in love with him, I prefer that kind of pain to thinking about what's going to happen when Mom sees my end-of-semester grades and realizes her dreams for me are dead.

So instead of dwelling on that, I watched Tyler. And as I watched, I noticed that he was heading toward the door out to the playing fields, and obviously if he went through that, I would lose sight of him. I don't know what came over me exactly, except that I really didn't want to go back to thinking about that history test or those chicken fingers. So I started moving. I stepped out of the line and I followed him.

It was drizzling a little outside, so there weren't many people around. I scanned the low wall and the steps where students usually gather at lunchtime, but I didn't see Tyler or anyone else. Then I turned and saw Tyler ducking down into a little passageway between the main school building and the auditorium.

I hurried toward where I'd seen him last, still with no fixed idea what I was doing or what I'd do if he spotted me. It's like I was on autopilot. That's when I heard the *click-clack* of heels on a small flight of concrete stairs, along with the soft thud of Tyler's sneakers. He'd been looking for Ada, of course. And now he'd found her.

From where I was, I could lean over a railing and see them both at the bottom of the stairs. Ada was wearing a short red trench coat that matched her nails. She slipped out of the rain under a little overhang and pulled out a cigarette and a book of matches.

"Dammit," she said in a low voice as one match after another went out. The wind had picked up. She was facing away from Tyler, and at first I thought she might not know that he was there, but then she said, "I don't suppose you have a lighter."

"I don't smoke," said Tyler.

"Of course you don't," said Ada, still not looking at him. Her straight blond hair fell like a curtain between them.

They stood together in silence a moment while Ada tried and failed to get another match to light. Tyler took a step forward. "I can help," he said. He leaned his body close to hers, rounding his shoulders to block the wind and blocking my view of her. After a moment, I heard her say thank you, and a plume of smoke rose to where I was standing. He didn't move.

"I said 'thank you,'" Ada repeated, more sharply this time.

"Don't be stuck-up," said Tyler. "I know what you are."

"Is that a fact?"

"I'll tell everyone."

"Be my guest," said Ada, not looking at him. Her phone trilled with a text message. "I've got to take this," she said.

"Okay."

"That was code for, 'Run along, now.'"

"Go ahead," he said. "I don't mind."

The phone trilled again. "Fine," said Ada, and she moved out from behind him, back into the rain. She started to walk up the stairs, but he reached behind him and grabbed her arm, tugging her back down to his level. "Ow," she said. "What's the . . . ?" But she didn't say anything else because he was kissing her.

"Hey," I cried out. Not stopping to think, I took the steps two at a time. "What are you doing? She said no."

Tyler stepped away from her, wiping his mouth with the back of his hand.

"No, she didn't," he said. "Who are you?"

At that point, my sudden attack of bravery wore off, and my throat closed over my voice. It's funny, because even then Tyler barely glanced at me. He kept staring at Ada until she said in a low, hard voice, "Get lost now. I mean it." At that he shrugged his shoulders, forced out a laugh, and wandered off toward the playing fields as if that had been his plan all along.

Ada's phone trilled again. "I've got to take this," she said, and she walked off in the other direction, leaving me alone in the rain.

I don't know exactly what to make of that whole scene. But I guess Ada doesn't really like Tyler.

I spoke to Ada again today. Or actually, she spoke to me.

I'd stayed away from her since our last interaction. I don't know why, but somehow I was embarrassed. I thought maybe she was mad that I interrupted what was going on between her and Tyler. And I definitely didn't want to see Tyler. So I did my best to stay out of sight, which is usually easy for me.

But Ada found me after school today. I was walking across the parking lot to the buses when she called my name. I was so surprised I didn't even answer. Ada Culver knows my name? It was hard to imagine, but she must have done some detective work after our last meeting.

I stopped and stared at her. She was standing by herself, away from the crowd, in a dun-colored coat with a cream fur collar that almost blended with her pale hair. She had her hands stuffed in her pockets, and she was shivering even though it wasn't that cold. I continued not to move, and eventually she approached and stood before me, maybe two feet away.

"Thank you," she said.

"For what?" I had thought of her before as beautiful and stunning, but now that she was close-up, I realized there was nothing unusual about her face or her body. She was skinnier and taller than me, but not statuesque. Her skin was pale, and a smattering of freckles on her slightly snub nose made her look almost wholesome. I had been fascinated before by her confidence, her coolness, but standing in front of me now, she seemed almost fragile. But that was fascinating too.

"The other day," she said. She pulled out a cigarette and lit it. She had a lighter this time. "Stuff like that . . ." She waved her cigarette vaguely. "We need to look out for each other."

We? I didn't know what she meant. Humankind? Women? Or me and her?

"It's fine," I said, and I turned to go.

"Why did you follow me outside?" she said abruptly.

I stopped again. "I wasn't following you."

She nodded as if she had half expected this answer. "You like Tyler," she said. It wasn't a question, so I didn't answer. She took a long drag. "A bit of advice," she said on her exhale. "Stay away from him."

I stared at her in surprise. Did she actually think I was a threat?

"You don't have to worry about me," I said.

"No?"

"Boys don't . . . do that to me."

"Lucky you."

I didn't say anything.

"You don't think you're so lucky," she said. "Is that it? You wanted it to be you he was mauling."

"No," I said quickly, but my hands were sweating. She was right. I hadn't even admitted it to myself, but there was a part of me that did wish it was me he had pushed up against that wall.

Ada shook her head, her hair catching what remained of the winter light. "You think that's what passion looks like, but it's not. Tyler's just a little boy, trying to be a big man." She dropped her cigarette on the pavement and crushed it under her heel. "Anyway, I should have said thank you the other day. So thank you."

"Sure," I said.

Ada turned away and walked toward a waiting car.

Wed, Nov 5

Screw this journal and screw Mom. I am so done with recording my pathetic attempts to distinguish myself for colleges, and I am really done with her nagging and demanding. I got second place overall at the swim meet today, but when I told Mom, she barely even looked up except to ask how the debate tournament went. Well, Mom, let me tell you: It was awful. I somehow got my notes out of order, and my opponent was really good, and the upshot was I didn't even place. Not that this is any surprise—I've never been good at debate. I hate public speaking. I never would have joined that stupid club except that Mark was awesome at it, of course, so

22

Mom naturally assumed that I should do the exact same thing.

How hard would it be for her to just say congratulations? Or nice job? Or maybe make a comment about how all my hard work in the pool paid off? But no. She has to fixate on the debate thing, which spiraled into a monster list of all my other shortcomings, until she cornered me into a two-hour lecture about what a worthless, terrible, disobedient child I am. Disobedient! That was the real slap in the face. All I ever do is obey. For as long as I can remember, I have done everything she asked, everything she told me to do, everything she wanted, up until and including this dumb journal. And what has it gotten me? Not a whole lot.

And the worst thing is, I don't even know why. Do I care about her approval? Do I even want it? Or is it just a failure of imagination? Maybe I let her direct every tiny aspect of my life because it's easier than thinking for myself, than actually deciding what it is I want and what's important to me.

Everything in my life has always been for her, from which classes I take to which activities I do to the food I eat and the clothes I wear. And I have never questioned any of it, but what's my reward? To be told that I've failed at being a dutiful daughter. The only thing I've ever really tried at.

Sometimes I wonder what she would do if she had a really bad daughter. It would blow her mind. I should do that, just to make her appreciate how good I've been all this time. Just let everything go, let myself be bad.

Oh, who am I kidding? I'd never have the guts to do that.

Thurs, Nov 6

I did it! I can't believe it, but I actually did something, well, bad today. I guess I am officially a bad girl now. And weirdly, the world didn't end. In fact, I seem to have gotten away with it.

I feel like an idiot for spending so much of my life being well behaved and obedient, terrified that if I ever did anything wrong, anything for myself, anything fun, everything would come crashing down around me. I'm not even sure what I thought would happen, but I had to believe there was some terrible punishment awaiting me, or else why would I keep doing all that stuff I didn't want to do?

And now I feel like that was all a big lie. The world doesn't work like that at all, and I don't have to live in constant fear of messing up. I can live a little, breathe a little. Make my own decisions. And it will be okay.

Even if I do wind up getting found out and getting in trouble, I don't know that I care. I wouldn't change anything about today, because it was amazing. Even if I get grounded for a million billion years and never see sunlight again, I won't regret today.

It didn't start that great, honestly. In my fit of rebellion last night, I decided not to study for my chemistry test, and taking the test without any preparation felt pretty bad. I even felt a little sick to my stomach, just thinking about having to turn it in with basically nothing on it. I never do that. Usually I'm freaking out if I think I might get anything less than a ninety, so the very thought of what a zero might do to my average made me break out in a cold sweat.

I started panicking right there in the middle of the test, and I guess I must have looked pretty bad, because the teacher asked me if I was feeling all right. I took that as my cue. I just said "no" and got up and ran out of the classroom. Part of me was sure he would come after me, but the decision was made for me pretty quickly by my stomach. So I just ran for the nearest bathroom and barfed into one of the toilets.

I felt a lot better after that, but I didn't know what to do with myself next. I really didn't want to go back to class and finish the test. But I didn't want to go to the nurse either. So instead I just hid out in the bathroom until I could go to my next class.

That's when Ada walked in.

She was wearing a wrap dress that clung to every line and curve of her figure. She gave me a quick look and said, "Hey," before starting to reapply her lipstick in the mirror. "Shouldn't you be in class?" she asked.

"Shouldn't you?" I countered.

She shrugged and returned her attention to the mirror. "I won't tell if you don't."

That seemed like the end of the conversation, but I didn't want it to be. I cast around for something else to say to her, but before I could think of anything, she started up again. She capped the top of her lipstick with a delicate pop, then turned to me and said, "Why is it you never wear makeup at school?"

"Me?" I said, as if there were anyone else she could have been talking to.

"You," she said. "I always thought . . . you and your friends. None of them wear makeup. I always figured it was because you were above it. You seemed to have more important things to worry about than looking pretty for boys."

That in itself was a revelation. Ada Culver, of all the people on this earth, had not only looked at me and noticed me before we ever spoke, but it sounded like she might have been a little jealous of me. It's weird to even write those words down. I can't really believe that it's true, but I don't know. In the moment, I was so shocked I couldn't even say anything.

"But now," she continued, "now I know you're just as boy crazy as anyone in this place. You want boys like Tyler Adams to like you. So why don't you try?"

"What do you mean, try?"

"You're a smart girl. You can figure it out. Take some of that brainpower you put into your classes and apply it to your looks. You could have ten Tylers if you wanted."

I shook my head. "It would take more than a coat of lipstick to make a boy like that notice me."

Ada looked me up and down, appraising. "You'd be surprised what lipstick can do. Come here."

I opened my mouth to ask why, or maybe to put her off, but then I realized I didn't want to, and I didn't care why. I pushed myself away from the wall and stepped toward her. She smelled like jasmine and tobacco.

"Tilt your head up," she said, "and relax your mouth."

One of her hands came up and rested just below my ear, steadying my head. With the other, she carefully smudged the waxy pigment around my lips. "There," she said. "What do you think?"

She stepped away from me, and for a minute I just stood there rubbing my lips together, acclimating to the strange feel of it. Then I turned toward the mirror. If I had been expecting a miraculous, Hollywood-style transformation, I didn't get it. I guess I had been, because I couldn't quite stop a bubble of disappointment from welling up inside me. It was still my face, still my boring, blunt haircut, still my broad swimmer's shoulders and practical clothes. But now ornamented with a slash of bright red. It was definitely striking.

"Hmm," said Ada. "Not really your color. But I have more at home. You should come over. I haven't played makeover in years."

Ada Culver was inviting me to her house? I couldn't quite believe my ears.

"When?" I said.

She gave me a funny look. "What's wrong with now?"

"But it's the middle of the school day."

Ada started to laugh but swallowed it back down. "Yeah," she said. "That's right." Not like she had forgotten, but like she had forgotten that might mean something to other people. She dropped her lipstick tube into her purse and turned toward the door.

"Wait," I said, and she stopped. I thought about my fight with my mom, how just once I wanted to show her what real disobedience was. And how I'd never had the guts to really do it.

"I . . . ," I said, hesitating for a moment on the edge of this new me. "Okay. Let's go."

We took the bus. I kept expecting someone to stop us and ask us what we were doing out of school in the middle of the day, but no one did. Maybe it was the lipstick. I don't know if it made me look more grown-up, but it made me feel more in control. Like I was wearing a mask, almost.

Ada's house wasn't at all what I'd expected. Based on her clothes and her phone and how she carried herself, I just assumed her house would be some big mansion with a pool and a housekeeper and a badminton court in the yard. But we got off in front of a small, shabby ranch house covered in pale yellow aluminum siding, with a big hole sliced through the screen door. Ada unlocked the door and let me in. The rooms inside were cramped and dark, with junk mail and celebrity gossip magazines strewn over every surface. I've never thought of myself as one of the rich kids, but it made my house seem like a palace. I mean, at least we've got two floors and a piano and the beautiful garden Mom works so hard on. Ada's house looked like no one really cared about it at all.

Ada showed me down a hallway to her bedroom. Clothes were heaped on every surface, as well as scarves and shoes and a pile of coats in the corner.

"Sorry," she said. "I don't usually have people over."

I hovered between the desk and the bed, still not sure what I was doing there. Ada stayed on the other side of the room, leaning against the doorjamb with her hands behind her back. She looked nervous. "It's kind of a dump, I know."

"No," I said, thinking of my room back at home. It was clean and neat, with every little piece of my life squared away into its proper place, wallpaper and bedding chosen without consulting me. It felt like a prison. "I like it. Is it okay if I . . . ?" I indicated the bed.

"Go ahead." She nodded. "You can just dump all that stuff on the floor."

I couldn't bring myself to do that, so I just pushed some of the clothes toward the other side of the bed and perched myself on the edge. She tugged out her desk chair. On the seat was a rat's-nest tangle of jewelry.

"Right, the lipstick," said Ada mysteriously. "Let's see what we have."

She pulled a shoe box out from under the desk and opened it. It was cluttered with all kinds of makeup, from samples to cheap drug-store tubes to stuff that looked really fancy.

"Hmm, purple could be dramatic," she said, "but maybe too gothy. Coral . . . No, all wrong for your skin tone. Maybe something with some brown?"

"Brown?" I said dubiously.

"It sounds like it would be ugly, but it's very sophisticated. I promise. Here." She held up the tube she had been seeking, uncapped it, and twisted it to reveal a deep, earthy russet. "This will be great on you."

She grabbed a tissue from a box on the dresser and carefully wiped the other color away, then replaced it with the darker hue. She sat back to examine her handiwork. "Beautiful."

"That might be an exaggeration," I mumbled.

She leaned closer to me, and I could smell her perfume again.

"Oh, I don't know," she said, brushing the bangs off my face. "You don't know it, but you could break a lot a hearts with those cheekbones."

"Very funny."

She raised an eyebrow. "I don't get the joke."

"Sure you do," I said, feeling frustrated. "It's me. I'm the joke, and you're the one laughing. I can't have a guy like Tyler any more than I can have a diamond bracelet or a . . . a unicorn."

Ada laughed. It was the first time I'd heard her laugh, and it was a jagged sound, like a machine that hadn't been used in a while.

"I don't know about the unicorn, but you could have Tyler if you wanted him, and the diamond bracelet too. But you're too smart for that, right?" I didn't answer. "Right? You saw what he was like. And now that you've seen, you know better than to think that's a prize worth fighting for."

I think I managed to nod. In any case, she gave me a brief smile.

"Here," she said, pressing the tube of lipstick into my

palm. "You should take this. It looks awful on me. Now you just need some clothes to go with that pretty face."

Her long legs took her from the bed to the closet in two strides. She started going through the piles of clothes all over her room and tossing things at me. It seemed crazy at first. . . . She's tall and skinny and I'm short and dumpy, but she said not to worry.

"It'll look different on you, but good." And she was right. I put on a dress I've seen her wear—a clinging navy knit with small brass buttons—and a part of me had a fantasy that it would magically turn me into her. It didn't, but when I stood in front of the mirror, it didn't look bad. I looked curvy, not dumpy.

"There you are . . . all dolled up for a night out on the town."

I laughed. "Not like I have anywhere to go."

That's when it hit me. It was two thirty, almost the end of the school day, and Mom would be expecting me home soon. Plus, I needed to figure out an unfamiliar bus route. "I need to get going," I said, heading for the door to her room. Then I remembered I was still wearing her dress. I went to take it off, but she stopped me. "Keep it," she said. "It looks better on you."

That was definitely the lie of the century, but I appreciated it. Even if it didn't look better on me than on her, it definitely looked better than any of the clothes I currently owned. I stuffed my school clothes into my swim bag and hurried off.

On the bus home, I couldn't help smiling to myself. I felt like I had finally figured out what friends were. Technically, Jenny and Eiko and the other geeks were my friends, but I didn't much enjoy the time I spent with them, and if we got together, it was only to study or work on a project. With Ada, it wasn't like that at all.

All afternoon I had been on an adrenaline high from skipping school and hanging out with the bad girl, but on that bus, my normal self caught up with me and I started panicking about what would happen when I got home. Would my mom know? Well, obviously, if I walked in with makeup on and someone else's clothes, that wasn't going to help my case.

I dug a tissue out of my bag and carefully swiped off all traces of the lipstick. Then I got off the bus a few blocks from home and changed into my usual clothes in a restaurant bathroom. By the time I got to my house, I was back to my normal self, and only a few minutes later than usual. Still, as I opened the door, my heart was in my throat, not knowing what might await me. I heard Mom call me as the door swung shut behind me. I found her in the den, playing mah-jongg on the computer.

"Someone called this afternoon," she said in Chinese. The school. They called to let her know I ditched class. My heart pounded in my chest so hard I was sure she could hear it.

"Check the voice mail," she said without looking up from her game.

That's when it hit me. Mom never answered the phone unless it was a familiar number—someone from our family or the Chinese community. She didn't trust her English on the phone with strangers, so she let the voice mail get it and had me or my dad listen to it when we got home. This was perfect! I nodded meekly, obediently, and went off to listen to the message. It was the school, reporting me absent for my third-through sixth-period classes. I pressed delete.

Thurs, Nov 13

Oh God, I've never been so humiliated in all my life. I'm such an idiot! Why did I ever get it into my head that I could be like Ada? Ada ... she's from a different planet from me. We're not the same species. As if a dress and some lipstick could change that!

All right, might as well record my foolishness, so I can read it over every day for the rest of my life as a reminder not to ever do anything risky again.

We had a swim meet. Remember when this journal was for tracking my success at things like swim meets? Yeah, well, forget it. I did terribly. I just couldn't focus at all. I don't know why; it just all seemed so unimportant.

Anyway, after my terrible swim, I was sitting there watching the boys get ready for the next event, dealing with pitying looks from the coach and a couple people on the team, and there was Tyler and . . . I know what Ada said. I know he's a creep, but he's just so incredibly perfect-looking. I haven't seen the whole world yet, but I swear there is no more beautiful physical specimen of masculinity to be found anywhere.

And that's when it came into my head . . . the most terrible idea in the universe. I remembered then and there that I still had Ada's dress and the lipstick she gave me in my gym bag, and I just thought, what if? What if I put it on? What if I got on the bus home tonight looking like . . . like . . . well, not like Ada, obviously, but like a person. Like a girl, instead of some invisible nothing, like I usually am. Ada said it. She said I could get Tyler if I wanted him. Well, goddammit, I want him, and if willpower and lipstick are all it takes, I have both of those.

So after the meet we were all getting changed, and I did it. I slipped on Ada's dress instead of my usual track pants and T-shirt. And I lined up with some of the other girls at the mirror to apply my lipstick. I made a mess of it, of course, because I'd never really done it before, and my hands were shaking with nerves. But eventually, by copying what I'd seen and felt Ada do, I managed a reasonable, not sloppy-looking mouth. Eiko, of course, gave me a hard time about it. She could

35

not have acted more shocked and appalled to see me in a dress. I guess it was more than just a dress. I mean, it doesn't have a whole lot in common with my recital dress. She was all, "What are you doing?" I didn't know what to say, so I thought about what Ada would do in that situation, and I ignored her.

When we got on the bus, I was so scared my knees were shaking. But I took a deep breath and got a grip on myself, and I walked right by Eiko and the empty seat next to her and went to the back of the bus. Obviously, it would have been ideal if I could have approached him alone, but I couldn't think of any way to do that, so I just kept moving forward, deeper and deeper into this terrible plan, letting the momentum of it carry me through.

Tyler was sitting at the back of the bus, surrounded by all his friends. They were laughing and talking and not paying any attention to me at all. At first. One by one, they started to notice me . . . the friends, that is. Not Tyler. Some of them just looked at me in confusion or surprise, but at least a couple of them were looking at me in a particular way. A way I'd only ever seen boys look at other girls. Girls who aren't me. But I wasn't interested in them.

I thought about saying something to get Tyler's attention, but I knew I wouldn't be able to come up with anything that didn't make me sound like an idiot. And Ada didn't need to do a bunch of talking to get people to notice her. If there's one skill she has mastered, it's smoldering silently until every eye in the room is drawn to her. So that's what I did: I tried to smolder.

It probably looked pretty ridiculous.

Eventually, Tyler took note of his friends not paying attention to him anymore, and he looked in my direction. Plan on target! Unfortunately, I hadn't thought the plan through at all beyond this point.

"What?" he said at last. Which, all things considered, is not an unreasonable thing to say to someone who is staring at you. But it wasn't exactly the conversational opener I was hoping for.

So I just kept staring at him. Smoldering. In silence. Like a complete idiot.

He stared back. I kept staring. He raised his eyebrows. I stood like a statue. Finally, he said, "Could you, uh, leave? You're kind of creeping me out."

That broke the spell. I turned around and went back to my seat. Eiko, of course, asked me what the hell was going on, but I just stared ahead of me the whole ride back and tried not to cry. What the heck has gotten into me? I definitely won't be trying that again.

Fri, Nov 14

I saw Ada again today. Well, that makes it seem like I just ran into her, like I did the other times. This time was a little different. I went looking for her. I found her pretty easily, not surprising, given how well I'd committed her habits to memory back when I was basically stalking her. At lunch she was lurking in one of her usual corners with a cigarette and her phone, wearing a closely fitted dress with a subtle golden shimmer.

"Hey," she said as I approached, as if it were the most normal thing in the world. As if we were actually friends. It threw me off a bit. But then I remembered how angry I was.

"You lied to me," I said without preamble. I had to get it out before I lost my nerve.

Ada looked up from her phone, surprised. Then she narrowed her eyes. I got the impression that she was willing to accept she had probably lied to me at some point and was just trying to figure out what particular untruth I might be referring to.

"You said," I went on, building steam. "You said that if I really tried, if I wore your clothes and your lipstick and did everything just like you, I could have him. Did you really think it would work? Or did you know all along exactly how hopeless it was and set me up so you could have a good laugh?"

Ada gave me a puzzled look. "I'm pretty sure I never said any of that."

I opened my mouth to object, then closed it again. I guess it was true that she hadn't said precisely that.

"What I told you," she said pointedly, "is that boys like Tyler are interchangeable. You don't need Tyler—you need someone else to put him out of your head." Ada's eyes moved back down to her phone, and I seemed to have been dismissed from the conversation. But just as I was turning to leave, she looked up again and caught me in her gaze.

"Hey," she said without elaboration. She cocked her head and looked me carefully up and down, as if considering something. Whatever she saw must have made up her mind. "What would you say to a date tonight?"

"With you?"

Ada gave me a strange look—surprised or amused, maybe. "A date with a man, not a boy."

I shook my head. "I really don't . . ."

"You'd be doing me a favor. I double-booked by accident."

My mouth went dry, and I had a feeling in my stomach like I get before a test.

"I don't think anyone in the world would confuse me for you," I said.

"It won't make any difference. He's a nice guy, and he'll like you. I promise. I wouldn't set you up with a jerk."

A million objections ran through my head. The last real date I had been on was more than a year ago, with a boy from the swim team, and Mom drove us to the movie and home again. There was no way she was going to let me go out with a total stranger who was out of high school. It was a completely insane idea. But what came out of my mouth was, "I don't have anything to wear."

Ada smiled. "I'll take care of that."

Fri, Nov 14, later

Writing this while I wait. What am I even waiting for? I don't know exactly, but Ada says not to worry. I don't know why I trust her, but I do.

I am sitting in a hotel bar at the convention center downtown, with a Coke in front of me. They put a lemon in it, but I fished it out. Sorry. That was a stupid detail. I'm just nervous, I guess. But writing calms me down.

I told Mom I was going to sleep over at Jenny's so we could work on our Science Olympiad project, and I went home with Ada after school. She found an outfit for me—a minidress with a fun geometric print—then fixed my hair and did my makeup. Not much, though. Too much would make me look older, she said.

"Isn't that good?"

"Don't be in such a rush," she said.

She took me to the convention center and went in with me. She ordered this Coke for me, in fact, and said something to the bartender before she brought it over to the table. This is all so mysterious.

Then she said she had to go.

"You're not going to stay and introduce me?"

"I told you, I double-booked. I really have to run."

"How will he know who I am?"

She smiled. "He'll know."

Then she gave me her cell number and told me to call her if I needed anything, or if I wanted to get out of the date, and she'd take care of it. "We have to look out for each other," she said, just like the other day. She gave me a kiss on the cheek. "Don't worry. You'll be fine."

Oh, someone just walked in! Is it him?

Sat, Nov 15

Wow. I kinda can't believe where I am right now. Or what I've done. Or how much I can't wait to do it again.

Last night . . . I'm not sure I even have the words. It was the most incredible night I've ever had. I've never been on a date like that with a boy . . . with a man before. I didn't even know dates like that were real. It was like something out of a movie.

I was so nervous in the beginning, looking around at every person who walked in, trying to figure out if they were looking for me, because I totally didn't believe Ada that the guy would just know. I mean, how could he know? But then, just as I was craning over my shoulder to look at a dude in a baseball cap leaning against the bar, a man slid into the seat across from me. I jumped a little when I realized what had happened.

"Um," was my opening conversational gambit.

"Hi," he said. He put out his hand to shake mine and he introduced himself as Damon. By that time, I had caught my breath enough to take in what he looked like. And he looked good. Really good. He was older, definitely not in high school, or probably college even. Maybe twenty-five? And he had dark curly hair and friendly brown eyes, and his smile . . . When he smiled it made me feel like I was the most important thing in the whole world.

He asked if I wanted to get out of there and suggested we go for a walk in Myrtle Edwards Park. We walked and looked at the ocean. I told him about how I've lived in Seattle my whole life but I've hardly ever seen the ocean even though I know it's nearby. It always seems to be a touristy thing to do, to go down to the waterfront, and I just never bothered. He told me he was kind of a tourist, though he's been to Seattle before, and he loves coming here.

He asked me about myself, and I told him all about swimming and how I used to love it but how it had gotten complicated recently, tied up with competition, so it just wasn't fun anymore. I almost slipped up and told him about how I tried to make a pass at a boy on the swim team, but I stopped myself. It occurred to me that that maybe wasn't appropriate first-date conversation.

Anyway, we talked and talked, and he was just really nice. So much nicer than Tyler. Ada was right about that. And I couldn't believe it, but he seemed really interested in me. No one has ever been that interested in me other than my mom. Mom always has to know every single little detail of my day, and I think she would dig into my brain to know every thought I have too, if she could. But she has her own reasons for that. It's more about control than caring.

So we were walking and talking about being tourists in our hometown, and I happened to mention that I'd never even been to the Space Needle. There was a class trip there when I was in first grade, but Mom kept me home that day because she didn't see the point in me wasting time on something "nonacademic." I'd always regretted it. I mean, it seems like a silly thing, but every time I see it, it's just another reminder of how I'm never allowed to do anything for fun.

And then Damon was like, "Let's go." I was like, what, to the Space Needle? He said yeah; he was getting hungry, and they have a restaurant up there. So he took me to dinner in the Space Needle! How cool is that? Wait, no, it gets better. Did you know that the restaurant spins around? So you can see views of the whole city while you eat dinner. Basically, it was the most perfect, most romantic thing ever.

We walked around some more after dinner, and the moon was so pretty and the weather was just perfect, and we sat on a bench and just talked and talked. Or rather, I talked and talked. Damon was mostly listening. I started to feel really awkward about the fact that I was talking so much, so I shut up. I wanted to give him a chance to talk, but he didn't. So I looked at him and he was looking at me and . . . This is a terrible analogy, but it was like a car crash, or how people talk about them, anyway. How time slows down and you see your life flash before your eyes. Because I just had this moment of, *Oh my God, he's going to kiss me*, and then he did!

It was sweet. Honestly, the only time I've kissed anyone before was in seventh grade at a birthday party, and it was awful, really awful. Really wet, and the boy was basically choking me with his tongue. I remember thinking at the time, *I don't ever want to do that again*. But this wasn't like that at all. He was really gentle and slow, and he just held me there like that until all I could think was that I wanted more. So I put my arms around his neck and pulled him closer.

After a while I felt his hand on my knee. It shocked me. Literally. It felt like a shock of electricity, and I pulled away from him. He immediately pulled back.

"I'm sorry," he said, and he looked really guilty. "I shouldn't have done that. I can take you home now."

But I realized that wasn't what I wanted at all. I didn't want to leave and go back to my boring, awful, normal life. More than anything, I wanted to keep kissing Damon.

So I said, "Don't stop." And I moved closer to him again and pulled him in for another kiss. We kissed for what felt like ages, and it was fantastic, but after a while this feeling came over me and I wanted more again. So I reached out and took his hand, which was nice but not quite what I wanted. So I put it back on my knee. Except not really on my knee . . . farther up. And we kept kissing, and I noticed his hand creeping higher and higher until my breath caught in my throat. He pulled back then and looked me in the eyes and said, "Is this okay?" I nodded. And he said, "Are you sure?"

I meant to say yes, but instead what came out was, "Please don't stop." That was really embarrassing and I blushed hard, but he just smiled.

"We're starting to put on quite a show for all the people walking by," he said. I think I must have turned super red at that. I started to pull away, but he said, "How about coming back to my hotel room?"

I hesitated a second, and he started babbling, apologizing and saying he shouldn't have said it. But the truth was, it was exactly what I wanted. And I told him so.

So we went back to his room at the hotel, and I couldn't believe how nice it was. I've stayed in only a couple roadside motels in my whole life, and they were nothing like this. There was an iPod docking station, a huge flat-screen TV, and a bowl of pretty little candies. I grabbed the bowl of candies and took it with me as I checked everything out. The best part was the bathroom—there were heated towel racks, a huuuuge tub, and another flat-screen TV so you could watch from the tub! I turned it on, and they were having a *SpongeBob* marathon and I got so excited. I haven't seen that show in ages. Plus, can you imagine watching *SpongeBob* while taking a bath? The whole concept made me giggle.

I called out to Damon to come see, like a big dork—as if he doesn't know his own hotel room. And he found me lying fully clothed in the bathtub, watching *SpongeBob* with a bowl of candies balanced on my stomach. I must have looked like an idiot, but he just stood in the doorway, grinning at me. So I was like, "What?"

"I don't know," he said. "I had kind of thought you might like to see the view from the window. Maybe have a glass of champagne."

"Oh," I said. "I'm sorry." I was embarrassed that I'd been so rude when he was being so nice. "I'll come and see."

Damon shook his head. "I guess we got enough views from Space Needle."

"I don't really like champagne," I admitted. "Do you want

46

some candy?" I lifted the bowl toward him, and he crouched down to take some.

"You're cute," he said.

I laughed. "No, you're cute."

"Is that right?"

And I couldn't believe he didn't know how cute he was. I wanted to show him, wanted to prove it to him. So I grabbed on to his shirt and tugged him closer to me and kissed him. He tasted like candy—there were still little bits of it in both our mouths, like little pockets of hard sweetness mixed into the soft kiss. It was awkward and uncomfortable and delicious and amazing. Eventually, he pulled back and asked if I thought the tub was big enough for two. Which it definitely was. I mean, it was huge, so I tugged on him a bit harder until he got into the tub with me. It wasn't exactly comfortable, lying in a dry tub with all our clothes on, but kissing him felt so good it didn't matter. Except then I guess his elbow or something knocked into the tap and turned it on, and suddenly we were both getting drenched with freezing-cold water!

I screamed at first, and then when I realized what happened, I couldn't stop laughing.

"Maybe that was a sign," said Damon.

"Did you want to stop?"

"Do you?"

I told him no, and he grinned and said, "Me neither. But maybe we need a change of venue."

He got out of the tub and put out a hand to help me up.

"And clothes," I said. Ada's sopping-wet dress wasn't the most comfortable anymore. Damon reached behind me and tugged the zipper down, then slipped the dress off me until I was standing there in my underwear. He wrapped his arms around me.

"That better?"

And that's when it really hit me—we were going to have sex. I guess it seems pretty idiotic that I didn't realize that earlier. In some sense, I guess I knew when he invited me back to his hotel room. But I didn't really believe it. It just seemed so unlikely that this guy really wanted me. I kept waiting for him to realize what a boring loser I am and tell me to leave. But when he took my dress off, that's when I realized—he was not going to change his mind.

Suddenly I felt nervous and awkward. Kissing was great, but sex was scarier. I started worrying that it would hurt, that Damon would expect me to know what to do, or that he would notice all the blobby bits on my body and get grossed out. But Damon put me at ease. He was undoing the buttons on his shirt, and he leaned forward to whisper in my ear.

"Are you scared?"

I held my breath and nodded a little. I could feel his breath on my neck and his lips on my earlobe.

"Do you want to stop?"

And even though I was nervous, I didn't want him to stop. I was still just so shocked that it was happening at all. I mean, I had more or less given up on this whole idea, on anyone ever wanting me—especially someone I actually wanted back. At school no one ever looked at me that way, and I got used to the idea that I was invisible to the world except as a geek and a nerd. But here I was, in a situation I always thought was reserved for other girls—prettier girls, cooler and more confident girls. At best, maybe one day I'd talk another virginal geek into it, or someone gross and desperate, someone selfish. But Damon was none of those things.

Of course I knew it wasn't love—I'm not naive. I don't expect him to marry me or send me love letters or whatever. But what we were doing . . . It felt good. Just kissing him felt better than I had thought it possibly could, and I would have been happy to keep kissing him all night. But if he's so good at kissing, it made sense that he'd be good at other stuff too.

So I kissed him again by way of answer, and I let him pull me over to the bed. He was really slow and careful and it did hurt at first, but it also felt really good. Afterward I felt sore in places I hadn't even realized existed, but he held me and stroked my hair until I fell asleep.

I guess it sounds super slutty, since I'd only just met him. But it felt right, and you know what? I don't regret it at all.

Damon was gone when I woke up, which at first made me a little sad, but honestly, it was kind of a relief too. Last night was so amazing, and I needed some time to process it all this morning. I feel like if he were around, odds are I would do something stupid or embarrassing or awkward that would sour the whole experience. And I don't want that. I want to cherish this night forever, no matter what else happens.

He did leave a really sweet note saying that he was glad he got to meet me and apologizing that he had to catch a really early plane this morning. And he told me to go ahead and have breakfast sent up to the room, on his tab! The other hotels I've stayed in were definitely the "coffee and doughnuts in the lobby" kind of places, but the room-service menu here has all kinds of amazing things. Would it be bad to order one of everything?

Oh! I have to call Ada and tell her all about it. I can't forget I really owe all of this to her.

Sat, Nov 15, later
Ada's not very happy with me.

I don't totally understand it, and she says it's not my fault, but apparently it's a huge deal that I had sex with Damon. I was so excited to tell her all about it! And I was pretty sure she wouldn't judge me. But I guess I misread the situation.

I sent her a quick text about it, and she immediately texted back asking for the hotel room. And said she was on her way over. I thought she just wanted to hear all about it, but when she got here, she was in a terrible mood.

She kept saying it was supposed to be just a date, a regular, normal date. She told him no sex, which I thought was really confusing. I mean, how is it her job to decide if I have sex or not? I thought only my mom was that controlling. Then she asked me if I was a virgin. I mean, if I had been. I was like, well, obviously. At that she groaned and put her head in her hands.

"I am so fucked," she said. I had no idea what she was talking about. "I told him you were probably a virgin and he was *not* to have sex with you," she went on. "I'm such an idiot. I should never have told him that. It's like telling a kid that there's candy hidden in the closet that he's not allowed to eat. God, that bastard. He's going to get me into so much trouble."

"What are you talking about?" I said, still totally clueless. "What trouble?"

"Damon knows better than to scam a freebie off Irma's girls," she went on, but she didn't seem to be talking to me. "And now Irma is going to think I made off with the cash."

"Cash?" I said. "What cash?"

"That's just it. There wasn't any! It was supposed to be a favor. I asked if he'd take a friend on a date, show her a nice time. As a friend."

Suddenly some things clicked into place.

"Wait. You mean Damon only took me out because you made him? He didn't even want to?" My chest felt hollow, but Ada just laughed.

"Believe me," she said. "He got what he wanted. It wasn't just a favor to me. It was . . . mutual. Damon likes girls the wrong side of legal, but he doesn't like to feel like a sleaze. His thing is to be Prince Charming, do a whole fancy date. And his fantasy is to deflower a virgin. So I told him I had a virgin for him, just like he wanted—for free. The only catch was, he couldn't sleep with you. No money changing hands—just a fun evening for everyone involved. All I wanted was to give your self-confidence a little boost, show you that you can do better than assholes like Tyler Adams."

I was trying to follow her explanation, but one detail kept tripping me up.

"Why do you keep talking about money?" I asked. "And who is Irma?"

Ada looked up at me with a guilty expression. "Irma is my boss." She took a deep breath and seemed to brace herself. "I turn tricks for a living," she said. "Damon is one of my old clients."

For a long time, I couldn't speak.

"Turn tricks," I said at last. "You mean you're a . . . a prostitute?"

I had to sit down on the bed. On the one hand, I felt like I'd never been so shocked in my life. But on the other, I felt like an idiot that I hadn't figured it out earlier. So many things about Ada suddenly made sense now. How she always seemed to have so much money even though her family didn't. Why she was on her phone constantly, even though she didn't have any friends. Why she looked so sophisticated and adult even though she was still in high school. Why she left school so often during the day. And why she knew guys like Damon she could fix me up on dates with.

Damon! I had a sudden fear that last night meant something very different from what I had thought.

"Did I just have sex with Damon for money?"

"No," said Ada. "That's what I've been trying to explain. I've known Damon for a long time now. I'd even call him a friend. I just wanted him to make you feel better about yourself, and I can't believe he dicked me over like this."

"Oh," I said, and suddenly felt washed in a wave of guilt. "That wasn't totally his fault."

"What do you mean?"

"It was . . . It was my idea, kind of. I mean, I may have sort of . . . pressured him."

Again, I thought back to last night, and so many things

53

seemed clearer. Why Damon had been such an incredible listener. Why he showed me such a good time. And why he seemed so hesitant to take the next obvious step. "He kept trying to back off, but I . . . I was the one who wanted more."

Ada looked at me like she didn't know whether to laugh or cry.

"You poor thing," she said. "You really feel responsible. Look, honey, you're sixteen. He's twenty-seven. You're a virgin, and he is . . . Well, he's about as far from that as they come. Believe me, you didn't force him into anything." Suddenly a new look of horror came over her face. "Wait," she said. "You made him wear a condom, didn't you? Oh God. Please say you did. I will fucking murder him if he—"

I reassured her that he did wear one, though again I felt a little guilty that it hadn't been my idea. It hadn't even occurred to me until he brought it out. What had I thought would happen? I really felt like an idiot that I hadn't even given a thought to pregnancy or disease. I was just so caught up in the moment.

Anyway, that calmed Ada down a little. She took my hands and asked me really seriously if I was okay and how I was feeling. I said I was fine, just a little confused.

"Do you need anything?"

I shook my head.

"Did you . . . ? Well, did you have any fun, after all?"

I couldn't help smiling at that. "Ada, it was the best night of my life," I said honestly. That made Ada smile back.

"Good," she said. "Don't worry, then. It will be fine. We'll just have to hope Irma never finds out about this little mix-up."

Tues, Nov 18

I just read over that last entry, and it feels like a dream I had. It's hard to believe that's something that really happened to me. I mean, in some ways it's hard to believe it happens at all. High school girls working as prostitutes? But it is really hard to imagine that I came in any way in contact with that world.

Not that I'm a prostitute! I never asked for nor accepted any money. Or was even offered any, for that matter. So really I'm just a sixteen-year-old girl who had sex with an older man. Which isn't that unusual. That's probably pretty normal, actually. It definitely isn't illegal. Oh wait. Yes, it is. I guess technically that's rape. Wow. How ridiculous that anyone would think what happened between me and Damon could possibly be called rape. I knew what I was doing! I'm not that innocent. Although I guess he did know a lot more about the situation than I did.

But whatever. It was great! I had a lot of fun, and I didn't do anything illegal, in any case.

But all that's over now, and it's back to regular life for me. It was kind of weird and twisted that Ada set the whole thing up for me, but also kind of . . . sweet in a way. I guess she really did see something in me that I didn't, and so did Damon. And the weirdest thing is, it worked! I still see Tyler all the time at swim practice, but I'm not obsessed with him like I used to be. My world's a little bigger now, and I can see he isn't the only good-looking guy in it (though he is still really good-looking—nothing's going to change that). But compared to Damon? He is a twerp and a loser.

The other nice thing is that I expected to be horribly embarrassed around him all the time now, ever since I did my weird staring thing at him the other day. And it's true that he and his friends sometimes laugh at me or make comments when I walk by, and the old me would have been devastated by that. But now I just can't find it in myself to care. There are more interesting things in the world.

Too bad I still have to go through the motions of high school. It's harder than ever to convince myself that history term papers and debate tournaments and my mom's nagging are important. But that's life, I guess.

Wed, Nov 19
I had a chemistry test today that I totally didn't know about. Oops. It was probably announced during one of the periods I missed because I was hanging out with Ada. I guess I really have let things slide.

So, obviously, I failed it. I mean, I wasn't exactly doing great in chemistry even before, and that was when I was taking notes and paying attention and reading the chapters three times before each test. I've never really had a mind for it. And now I'm skipping classes and fudging my way through the homework and zoning out so bad that I don't even realize there's a test coming up. Honestly, I don't know how I'm going to come back from this. I used to calculate my average each time I got a B on a test and compute how well I needed to do on the remaining tests to bring it up to an A. But given my last couple of tests, that's just not possible anymore. Maybe if I got perfect scores on everything for the rest of the semester, I could still get a low B, but what's the point? Mom will still be furious. Stanford won't even look at me. It's hard to see how it's worth the constant struggle.

There's a part of me that has always wondered . . . what would happen? What if I just let go and stopped worrying over every little thing? But I guess that's pretty much what I'm doing now. It's weird—it's like, instead of being an active participant in my own life, I'm just watching it like a movie. Waiting to see what happens to me.

Fri, Nov 21
So it turns out that once you've decided to stop caring about your classes, school gets really boring really fast. I've spent so

much of my life drowning in pressure and anxiety, and I guess I always assumed that people who didn't have that must be happy and relaxed all the time. I never imagined how depressing it would be to just . . . exist.

Even eating lunch with my old friends just feels impossible now. Today Jenny and Eiko were talking about our chances for Academic Decathlon this year, and they asked my opinion and I had nothing to say. I couldn't even really follow what they were talking about. The looks they gave me . . . It would have been embarrassing, if I cared at all.

Sun, Nov 23

I'm so bored.

Not just bored in this specific moment, from not having enough to do. God knows I have plenty to do. . . . In theory, I have tests to study for and papers to write and math team competitions to prepare for and helping Mom around the house, if I ever finish the rest of it. There is plenty of stuff to occupy my time. But I can't bring myself to do any of it, and none of it makes me less bored.

I can't stop thinking about that night with Damon. I can't stop wishing my life were more like that and less like this. It's like now that I've tasted that life, it is really hard to go back to my normal world of Mom picking on me and nagging me and never being satisfied with anything I do. And things between us are worse than ever now that I've pretty much stopped trying at all. My grades are plummeting. Half the time I don't even bother going to my activities. I haven't practiced the piano in ages, and as a result, every day when I come home from school, I get the same lecture about what a disappointment I am and how I am bringing shame on the family and will never amount to anything. I could bring real shame on this family if I wanted to! Maybe I should, just to show her. Mom is so sheltered. She has no idea what's out there.

I think a lot about Ada, too. Not that I don't see her. I mean, we're still friends, and sometimes I run into her in the halls and bathrooms at school. But I get flustered and don't know what to say. Her life is just so much more interesting than mine.

The other day she suggested we go shopping or something, and that sounded amazing. She always looks so glamorous and stylish. Maybe she could help me figure out how to do that too. But it's not like I have any money. It's kind of ironic, actually. Ada's family doesn't seem to have much money, but she personally has a lot of cash to spend, thanks to her work. Whereas my family is a lot more well-off, but that makes no difference in my life. I'm not like those rich kids with Daddy's credit card. I have to ask my parents to buy me things if I want them, and then they get to decide whether what I want is worth spending money on or not. Usually not. It's just another way they control me.

I can just imagine asking my parents for money to buy sexy boots or a gorgeous camel coat like Ada's. They'd think I was joking.

So in the meantime, Ada and I have less and less in common, and she has less and less reason to waste any time on a loser like me. And pretty soon the one bright spot in my life will disappear and it will all be nothing but drab and gray.

Maybe if I got a job? Then at least I'd have some cash I could call my own.

Sun, Nov 23, later

Well, forget the job idea. First of all, Mom totally did not go for it. I tried to use the angle that college applications ask about work experience, and it would show a sense of responsibility and hard work, but she wasn't having it. She said the last thing I needed was another thing taking my time and focus away from my schoolwork and my activities. She said maybe if I brought my grades up, she might think about it, but I don't see that happening anytime soon. Because the truth is, my grades lately are even worse than my mom realizes, and I'm just waiting for report-card day, when the whole truth comes out.

Not that I care that much. I mean, what can she really do? She can yell and complain and berate me all she wants. It can't be much worse than what I'm putting up with now.

And then the other thing is, even if I could talk my parents into it, I don't know if it would even be worth it. The only job I could possibly get would be part-time at minimum wage, and it would take me forever to save up any serious money. By the time I could afford a shopping trip with Ada, she would have forgotten all about me. Plus, they seem like kind of a drag. I mean, do I really want to spend hours every day mopping floors and scrubbing toilets? That sounds even worse than the stuff I currently have to do.

It all just feels so hopeless right now. Everything in my life is dull and pointless, and I can't even think of anything to look forward to. It's just a vast expanse of nothing, from here until forever.

Mon, Nov 24

It's the middle of the night, but I can't sleep. My brain won't shut down because there's this thought buzzing around in it—a totally crazy thought. But maybe if I write it out on paper I'll see just how ridiculous it is and my brain will finally leave it alone.

What if I did what Ada does? No, that's not good enough. I have to be able to say it. Okay. What if I became a prostitute? What if I were a whore?

Okay, see? Ridiculous! Crazy. I could never do that. That life isn't for girls like me.

Ada does it. But Ada's not like me. But could I ever be like Ada? I used to think no, definitely not. I remember when Ada seemed like she belonged to a different species. But it's not like that anymore, is it? We're friends. We share clothes. I look good in her clothes. And she herself said that I could be like her, if I wanted. I wonder if she was serious.

Back then I was a virgin and she was not. And that seemed like an unbridgeable gulf. But I'm not a virgin anymore—already I'm more like her. Damon wanted me, thought I was pretty. Thought I was sexy. A couple months ago, I couldn't even dream that. If Damon wanted me, other men probably would too. So I could do it. In principle.

But it's still nuts. I mean, what about my parents? Just imagining the look on Mom's face if she found out . . . She wouldn't believe it. She would never think me capable of such a thing. Because I'm not. Right? My mom should know.

But then, what does Mom know about me, really? I spend my whole life doing the things she expects of me, but is that who I am? I guess it is, in a way. I mean, you are what you do, right? But I'm not exactly happy with who I am right now. If I decided to do something different, something really crazy, would that make me a different person? Would I like that person better?

If she were more like Ada, then yes—I would like her better. Like me better.

And then there's the money. That would be nice, wouldn't it? I don't know. My family's not poor, like Ada's, so why should money be so important to me? It's not like there's a ton of fancy things I want to buy. But money isn't just about getting stuff. Having my own source of income would feel like ... freedom. Independence. Right now I have to do whatever my parents want because I'd basically die without them. But if I had my own money, I could make my own choices.

Wow. Am I really considering this?

I'm sure in the morning I'll see what a terrible idea this is and drop it completely. But it's a nice fantasy for right now.

Tues, Nov 25

I'm excited. I shouldn't be, but I am. This is a bad idea, but honestly, who cares? I'm nervous and scared, but at least I'm feeling something. My whole body is buzzing, and it's partly fear and surprise at myself, but it feels better than all that dead nothingness before.

I didn't mean to say anything. I didn't think I was seriously considering it. But at lunch today I was sitting alone, eating a sandwich, thinking over the whole concept, not quite ready to let it go yet. But then Ada slid onto the bench across from me and asked me what I was thinking about. And I just blurted it out!

"I want to do it," I said, as if she'd been listening in on my thoughts for the past twenty-four hours.

"What?"

"I want to be a . . ." I hesitated over the rest of the sentence. Not because I wasn't sure, but because I didn't know the right word to use. I didn't want to accidentally give offense. "Do you think that I could do what you do?" I said.

Ada raised her eyebrows.

"Have sex," I clarified. "For money."

Ada blew out a long breath. "Shit," she said.

"You don't think I could do it? You think people wouldn't want—"

"It's not that." She pulled her coat tight around her, a dark expression on her face. "I shouldn't have told you. I was afraid at first that this might happen, but then I thought, no way, not her. She would never be interested in—"

"Why not? Why shouldn't I be? You think I want to be an invisible geek my whole life?"

Ada shook her head. "It's not what you think. Damon . . . they're not all like that. They're not at all like that. Damon was the worst possible introduction I could have given you to this business."

"I know that," I said, smiling a little. "I'm not an idiot, Ada. I have actually thought about this. I know it's not all dinners at the Space Needle."

She frowned. "You don't understand."

But I do! I mean, maybe not completely. Of course not completely—how can I understand something I've never experienced? But how can I learn without experiencing it?

"Do you want to quit?" I asked her.

"No," she said slowly.

"Is anyone forcing you to keep doing it?"

"No, but I—"

"If it were really that bad, you would quit, wouldn't you?"

Ada nodded, a little uncertainly. "But it's not that simple. You don't know—"

"How can I know if I don't try it? And if I don't like it, I can stop, right?"

Ada relaxed a little. "Yeah. You could always back out, if you wanted." She didn't look totally convinced, but she stopped fighting me. And when I pressed a little more, she agreed to introduce me to Irma. She said after that it would be between me and Irma and out of her hands.

I can't believe it. I can't believe I'm really doing this! I'm not sure I even recognize myself.

Wed, Nov 26

Ada just called. My big meeting with Irma is today! I'm so nervous and excited. I wanted to go home first to change. I'm worried that if I don't look really pretty, Irma won't want me. But Ada said not to worry about that. Irma is sending a car for me! I really can't decide if I am more nervous or excited.

Ada just reminded me *not* to mention anything that happened with Damon. I still don't quite understand why that's such a big deal, but I can do that. Okay, I have to run.

Wed, Nov 26, later

Well, I have a job! Kind of. I still have to wait until I get scheduled for my first date, and of course I can't get paid before then. But Miss Irma took me on! I feel . . . relieved, I guess.

One thing I definitely didn't expect: Miss Irma (that's what everyone calls her to her face) came here from Taiwan, just like my parents. She's probably about their age, too. Oh, wow. What if they've met? Given the size of the Chinese community here, it's not impossible. I definitely don't want to think too much about that, though. Let's keep those worlds separate.

It was surreal because Miss Irma speaks English with an accent that sounds a *lot* like my mom and all my aunts. I mean, obviously her English is much better. She's been doing business in English for decades now. So more like my dad, in that way. She speaks very carefully, slowly, and her sentences are always correct, but the accent is still there.

I can't even describe how weird it is, because Miss Irma is

like the complete opposite of my parents in every significant way. She is not obsessed with me going to college and doing all my homework and stuff like that. But it's not just that. Everything about her seems so much less rigid and controlling. It's kind of a revelation to meet someone Chinese who isn't a doctor or an engineer or a scientist or some other "acceptable" successful career, like my parents' friends are. Miss Irma has made her own success, in a completely original way.

It made me feel like maybe there are more options open to me than I thought. Not that I necessarily want to do what Miss Irma does when I grow up, but I'm starting to see that I don't have to limit my dreams to the ones my parents consider acceptable. I can follow a different, less-obvious path, if I want to.

Irma's office wasn't really what I expected either. It was in a big anonymous high-rise tower downtown, mixed in among dentists and lawyers and gynecologists. Her sign in the lobby was very discreet, and you would never have guessed anything at all about her line of work from it.

Even once you got upstairs into the reception area, it still felt a lot more like a doctor's office than like a . . . well, a whorehouse. It's all pastel wallpaper and tasteful paintings and fluorescent lighting. I figure this can't be where Miss Irma meets her clients. I can't see anyone being turned-on by that decor.

Anyway, there was a receptionist, a pretty woman named Anne who told me to wait a few minutes and then eventually let me in to Miss Irma's office. She was sitting behind a desk, and, again, I couldn't help a weird shiver of recognition because the layout of the room and the desk and everything were so much like my dad's office at the hospital.

Miss Irma was friendly and smiled a lot, but the whole thing felt much more formal and professional than I was expecting. She was wearing a well-tailored gray tweed suit and a fussy perfume that filled the whole room with notes of lotus and plum. The only hint that she wasn't an ordinary businesswoman or bureaucrat was a pair of pearl-gray stilettos so high they made my feet ache just to look at them.

She asked me a bunch of questions about myself and my family (but nothing too personal), and she asked me how I learned about her operation. I was careful not to say anything about Damon. I just said that Ada was my friend, and I learned about it from her. Miss Irma seemed to accept this, and she told Anne via her intercom to add my name to her appointment book.

Then she asked me what were the best times for me, and I sort of slipped and said, "I can't do nights anymore." I was thinking about my night with Damon, but obviously I can't tell my parents I have an overnight study session every time. I knew

I'd messed up the minute it came out of my mouth, but I was hoping Irma wouldn't notice. But she's sharp. She picked up on it right away.

"Anymore?"

"I can't do nights," I repeated, trying to sound confident. "My parents would cause problems. It's easier to get away from school."

Miss Irma nodded and I breathed an internal sigh of relief.

"And your name?"

I repeated my name, even though I'd already introduced myself, and she gave me a sharp look over her reading glasses. "Not your real name. Never give a client your real name. You need a working name."

She tried to get me to come up with one on the spot, but I blanked completely, and after about half a minute, Miss Irma just sighed and said, "Sleep on it. You can let us know later." She made a few more notes in a big book on her desk, then looked up again. She told me I'd get a text in a few days, most likely, setting up my first appointment. Then she went over some ground rules:

> 1) Never accept money from the clients directly. Never discuss money with the client. All payment goes through Miss Irma.

2) Never discuss money with the other girls. Money talk is bad for morale, and Miss Irma doesn't like settling fights.

3) Never discuss clients with anyone. Spilling secrets is the fastest way to lose not just one client but all of them.

4) Never do anything you don't want to do. If a client asks for something that makes you uncomfortable, tell Miss Irma. Someone else will do it.

5) Safety first. If you feel unsafe, leave. Tell Miss Irma what happened as soon as possible.

6) If you are unhappy working for Miss Irma, you are free to quit at any time.

She asked me then if I understood everything. I said yes, and that was basically it! It was kind of anticlimactic, actually. I'm not sure what I was expecting, to be honest. Someplace with red shades on the lamps and mostly naked girls draped all over the furniture?

Toward the end she asked me if I had any questions, and for a moment I completely blanked and was about to shake my head no. But then I realized that actually yes, I had a ton of questions. The most obvious one being, what do we get paid?

Miss Irma smiled politely at this.

"Ada did not explain? It depends on the situation. Depends on the client, time of day, and nature of request. You leave that kind of thing to me."

"Oh," I said, feeling a little confused.

"Don't worry," she said, still smiling. "Everyone is paid fairly."

I was annoyed not to be able to get a more concrete answer out of her, but it's true that Ada had never complained about the money. It seems like a strange way to do business, but it can't be that bad or people wouldn't go along with it, right?

After that, all that was left was for me to check in with Anne. She had me pose against a bare wall for a quick photo, then handed me a pink phone just like Ada's.

"I already have a phone," I told her.

Anne explained that I needed a committed phone. One that Miss Irma controls. She doesn't like when the girls get their service cut off or their numbers changed. She needs to know that she and the clients can get in touch with us. Anne said it would take a day or two to charge and activate, but once it was all set, I should just wait for a text letting me know about my first appointment.

This is all so weird but exciting. It's like a strange dream, or something that's happening to someone else. Maybe once I do my first date, it will start to feel real.

Sat, Nov 29

Still no word from Irma. I'm starting to get nervous.

I'm not even sure what I'm nervous about. Part of me is afraid she's changed her mind and won't ever text me, and another part is terrified that she will. Sometimes I lie awake in bed thinking, *What am I getting myself into? Am I prepared for this at all?* I mean, I've had sex exactly once. Am I qualified to be a professional? Or is that a silly thing to ask?

What if it's weird and awful? What if I panic at the last minute and can't go through with it?

Yesterday I made Ada talk to me a bit about her experiences, to help calm my nerves. I made her describe an average date for me and what the guys are like and what they ask for. That helped a bit. Plus, she reminded me that I can always say no at any time. I can always turn around and leave if I'm not comfortable.

It helps to know that Ada has been through all this before. I want to be like her. I can be like her. I want to know something of the real world and not learn everything from books. I look at Ada, and I want all the experiences that made her what she is, even the bad ones. I can do it.

Mon, Dec 1

I got the text! I waited for ages. It felt like it was never going to happen. But I guess I have a client? This is all so weird. My handwriting is awful because I'm shaking a little, and I don't even know if it's fear or excitement. I mean I'm scared, but for the first time I feel like I'm living my own life and not just following someone else's path. Maybe this is a huge mistake, but it's *my* mistake and no one else's.

Miss Irma's car is coming for me at the same spot where I've seen Ada get picked up. That's basically all I know right now. I hope my dress is okay! (It's one of Ada's.)

Mon, Dec 1, later

I'm back from my date. I don't know what to say about it.

It was fine. It was . . . fine.

It wasn't fine.

I don't know. I feel like an idiot. Ada warned me. She told me most of my dates wouldn't be like Damon, and I heard her and I understood. I thought I understood. I knew they wouldn't all be as handsome as Damon or as kind. Or as young. But I thought . . .

I feel dumb even saying this, but I thought . . . at least they would appreciate me. Even if they were old and unattractive, they would at least make me feel sexy and wanted. But this guy . . . It's not that anything terrible happened. I didn't get hurt. He wasn't cruel. But I don't even know his name! I mean, I understand why people might not want to give their names, but not even a fake name. He was just so distant.

He had a drink in his hand when he came to the door, and I smiled and started to introduce myself when I realized I still hadn't thought of a fake name. So I was standing there with my mouth open like an idiot, trying to think of what to say, but I guess it didn't really matter, because he just grunted and turned his back on me. He didn't tell me his name or offer me a drink or tell me to take a seat or anything. So I just stood there. Eventually, he said, "What are you waiting for?" He was probably in his fifties, kind of fat, and wearing a nice collared shirt with gym shorts underneath, which was weird. He definitely did not turn me on.

At that moment, with everything so different from what I was expecting, I nearly turned around and walked out the door. But I knew if I did that, Irma would never book me for another date at all. I thought, this has to be a test. I don't even know if that's true, or if this guy was just the luck of the draw, but somehow it helped me to think of it that way. If there's one thing I know how to deal with, it's tests. Just focus and take deep breaths and do your best.

I did what he told me to, and I tried to do it well, though there was some stuff he wanted that was, well, more difficult than it looks in movies and stuff. But I think the worst thing is that through the whole thing, I had no idea if I was doing a good job or what I did well and what I did badly. The man was totally expressionless the whole time. It kind of hurt my feelings.

God, what a stupid thing to say. As if this is about my feelings! It doesn't matter what I want. It's about the client, not me.

Anyway, I guess it must not have been too terrible, because when I was done, he gave me a tip. Twenty bucks. I used it to get a cab home, because Irma's cars only take you to the appointment; they don't pick you up at the other end. We're on our own for that.

Now I'm pretty sore. But at least I'll get paid soon. It's funny. Now I can't remember why I was so eager for money.

Mon, Dec 1, later

I feel a lot better. Dumb, but so relieved. I just spoke to Ada. I hadn't planned to, but she called me, knowing that today was my first time. My first time for real. At first she just congratulated me, but I guess something in my voice must have given away how I was feeling, because she asked how I was and sounded really concerned.

I didn't mean to tell her. I didn't want her to feel responsible. But before I even knew what was happening, it was all spilling out of me, and I was sobbing into the phone. I told her I hated it. That I felt gross and used and like I wasn't even human. I asked her if that was normal and she laughed, though I don't think it was very funny. She said yes, that's normal. It's part of the gig.

I asked her how she put up with that, and she sighed and didn't say anything right away. Then, just as I was beginning to think we'd lost our connection, she said, "It isn't always like that."

"You mean like with Damon?" I said.

"Damon's great," she said. "But no, that's not what I mean. What I mean is, sometimes what gets you through is . . . human connection. Even with someone who is gross-looking and kind of rude, sometimes you get just a moment, a brief glimpse of the person as a person. And you think, I have a chance to make this person feel good right now. And it might be the only good feeling he has in the next month."

"But how do you know . . . ?"

"You don't. You never know. And maybe it's all a fantasy. Maybe the men are a fantasy to us as much as we are to them. Maybe there's no decent person under it all who needs you.

Maybe they are all dickbags. But you have to tell yourself something. I mean, there has to be something that gets you through it, week after week."

I thought about that for a while . . . tried to picture telling myself that story and believing it because I had to.

"Ada," I said after a while.

"Yeah?"

"I don't think I want to do it again."

I cringed as I said it, certain that she would be angry or disappointed or resentful. Angry, maybe, that I was passing judgment on the life she is living, or disappointed to lose a friend who understood her life, or resentful that I have the option of quitting and maybe she feels like she doesn't. But I didn't hear any of that in her answer.

"Good," was what she said, and she breathed out a heavy sigh that sounded like relief. "When you told me you were interested, I wanted to kick myself. I never meant to draw you into this."

"You're not upset?"

"Honey, no," she said sweetly. "It happens a lot. Loads of girls quit after their first date. It's fine."

I felt relieved too after that. I should have felt bad, giving up on this fantasy and going back to my normal life. Or embarrassed that I had given up so easily, after just one kind of crappy date that wasn't even that bad. But I think I'm doing the right thing. Even debate tournaments and chemistry tests don't sound so bad compared to the dead-eyed way that man looked at me.

Tues, Dec 2

Ada reminded me today that I still need to pick up my payment for my date. I asked if she would just do it for me so I wouldn't have to see Miss Irma again, but she said they don't like to do that because of that thing where no one's supposed to know what the others are earning, so I have to get it myself or just abandon it. I could do that, I guess. Wouldn't that make it better? If I don't take the money, I'm still not a whore.

But the man already paid the money, so maybe it doesn't matter. Besides, that feels almost worse in a way, if I did those things with that man for nothing. So I guess I'll go, even though it means cutting class again so I can go with Ada. I definitely don't want to go alone.

Cutting all this class is becoming a problem, though. At lunch Eiko asked me why I wasn't in French the other day. Awkward. I didn't know what to say, so I just mumbled something about not feeling well.

I really need to start putting more effort into school again. I've blown off so much lately, I think this semester may be a lost

78

cause. But as long as I don't flunk anything, maybe I can have
a fresh start next semester? Stanford is off the table (not that it
was ever a likely outcome), but that doesn't mean all hope is lost.
Right? I just need to buckle down.

Thurs, Dec 4

Went to pick up my fee today. It wasn't that bad. Well, the going
wasn't that bad. I didn't even have to see Miss Irma, which was
great. I don't know why I'm scared of her, since she's never been
anything but kind to me. Maybe it's because of the way she
reminds me of my mother. I just have this irrational fear that
if I tell her I'm quitting, she'll look at me the way my mom did
when I told her I wasn't going to play violin anymore: as if I had
simultaneously slapped her across the face and broken a family
heirloom.

But anyway, that part was fine because apparently Miss
Irma does not hand out the money. I guess maybe I should
have guessed that. We just went up to Anne's desk and gave our
names and she handed us each an envelope.

But the not-so-good part was when I got outside and
checked the envelope. First I thought there had to be some kind
of mistake. I'm not exactly an expert in the going rates for call
girls, but I wouldn't be doing much worse at those minimum-
wage jobs I was looking at.

I freaked out a bit at Ada. Not that it was her fault, but it did feel like kind of a betrayal, that she and Irma had refused to give me any solid numbers but both let me believe the pay would make everything worth it. But Ada calmed me down. She said she forgot to warn me—the first envelope is always skimpy, because of all the setup costs. Like apparently I have to buy my own phone (even though I already had a perfectly good phone). And we all have to pay Anne's and the driver's salaries. And Ada says they take that in a monthly sum, instead of per date.

That still seems kind of unfair to me, but Ada says they only charge you if you're working. If you didn't take any dates the month before, you don't have to pay in. So at least I'm not going to wind up owing money now that I've decided to back off.

Still, it sucks that I'll never get to see any real money from this, even though I did the work. Now I just have this stupid phone.

Oh, that reminds me. I was going to turn in my phone when we went today, since I'm not going to work for them anymore, but I was so shocked by the envelope that I forgot all about it. So now I've got this phone. Do I go back tomorrow and deliver it then? I really don't want to go back. Is it wrong to keep it? I mean, I did pay for it.

I guess I'll just hang on to it for now.

Tues, Dec 9

Things are getting back to normal. That is to say, boring, but that's okay. I'm trying really hard to catch up as much as possible in all my classes, and that's draining all my energy for the moment. I've pretty much stopped all my activities for now, because I just can't with all the schoolwork. I expected Mom to give me a huge hassle about that, but she seemed to agree. School comes first, she said.

I've even quit swimming, which sucks, because I really do love that. But there isn't any point in showing up when I can't swim competitively right now. My head's just not in it. But I don't know, maybe I should start hanging out at the local YMCA or something, just to get in the water from time to time. Could be fun.

There is one other thing that is bothering me a bit. More than it should, maybe. It's this damn phone. I still have it, and I feel it weighing on me. The phone doesn't know that I've quit, and neither does Miss Irma. And neither does Anne, I guess. Which means my name is still in the appointment book, and I could get a call for a new date at any moment. Ada says all I have to do is say no. It's no big deal. People say no all the time, for all kinds of reasons—they're busy, or on their period, or have a cold or whatever.

And anyway, the phone hasn't rung. I haven't gotten a

peep out of it since my date. I wonder if that means the guy complained about me, so now Miss Irma doesn't even want me anymore.

I have no idea why that should bother me, of all things. I should be thrilled, if that's the case. But I guess even whores have pride.

I wish it didn't weigh on me, though. That one of these days the phone is going to buzz and it's going to be a text from Miss Irma setting me up on a date and it's going to make the whole rotten experience come flooding back. I kind of just want to pitch the phone into the ocean and never think about it again, but I have a feeling Irma wouldn't be too pleased about that. And I don't think I want to make an enemy of her.

Thurs, Dec 11

I got a text today—on the pink phone. But it wasn't Irma texting, and it wasn't Anne.

It was Ada.

That made the whole thing very different from what I was expecting. What I was worrying about. All it said was, *I need a favor. Call me.*

I called her right back, of course.

"I need your help," Ada said as soon as she picked up the phone. She sounded anxious.

82

"What is it?" I said. "What's the matter?"

Ada took a deep breath. "I know you're out of the business," she began, "and I really didn't want to have to do this. . . . Believe me, I'm the last person who wants to drag you back in. But I'm in a jam."

"I'll do it," I blurted out.

"What?" said Ada. "But I haven't even told you what it is yet."

"I know," I told her. "But if you're in trouble, I want to help. Whatever it is. Like you said, we need to look out for each other."

Ada didn't answer a moment as she weighed this over. "I did say that, didn't I?" she said at last. She took a breath. "Okay, then, if you're sure. Meet me at the pickup spot. I'll explain in the car."

Fri, Dec 12

Wow. I have so much to tell. I'm not sure how to put it all in words. And some stuff I'm not sure I want in words. . . .

But what does it matter? I had fun.

I can't believe I gave up so easily before. Maybe I just need to stick close to Ada. . . . She's my lucky four-leaf clover in all this. I wish she ran this business instead of Miss Irma. Then it would all seem like no big deal.

But I'm getting ahead of myself, and I do want to get all this down.

I met Irma's car outside the school and slid in next to Ada. She looked stunning as always in a charcoal dress with red detailing, which somehow made my patterned top and skinny jeans seem plain and boring. Ada explained then what the favor was about: A client wanted two girls at once.

I breathed a huge sigh of relief when she told me that, which I think surprised Ada. I guess she expected me to be shocked, and . . . Well, okay, it is a little weird. It's not exactly something I ever pictured myself doing. But when she told me she needed a favor, I figured it must have something to do with Miss Irma, and I assumed she double-booked again or something. So I thought I was going to have to do another date on my own, which made me really anxious. I mean, I'd do anything to help out Ada, but I really wasn't excited about that.

So when she told me what she needed and I realized that she'd be by my side and I didn't have to go into this alone . . . That was just so much better than what I'd been picturing. I was still nervous, but I felt like nothing that bad could happen as long as Ada was there.

Turns out Miss Irma had set up the date for Ada and another girl, Jen, who Ada's friends with, but Jen couldn't do it today. I wanted to know why, and at first Ada tried to be vague, but then she stopped herself.

"No, you know what?" she said, almost to herself. "You

should know what happened to Jen. I want you to know."
She turned and looked at me very seriously, her eyes dark and
stormy. "Jen has a drug problem. She was doing smack last night
even though she knew she was working today and knew I'd be
furious with her. And I am. Not about the work, though." She
sighed. "It's only because I worry." Ada paused a moment to
collect herself, then went on.

"She was strung out this morning and could barely stay
awake. Then her asshole roommate convinced her that the
best way to deal with this problem was to snort a bunch of
Ritalin. Jen should know better, given what happened to Ella
last year. . . ."

Ada shook her head in sorrow and disbelief, but all these
people were little more than names to me. Suddenly, she
grabbed my hand, and the grip in those bony fingers was
surprisingly tight and forceful.

"You have to promise me," she said. "I mean it. Never get
mixed up in that stuff, okay? Don't kid yourself that you can
handle it. It will destroy you. You have to keep your head about
you in this business or it will eat you up."

None of this meant much to me. The closest I ever came to
drugs was when my parents let me have a sip of champagne at a
cousin's wedding, or the day they legalized marijuana here and I
smelled something weird and pungent when I walked near the

park on my way home from the bus stop. That world didn't seem to have much to do with me. But I tried to return her serious look while I nodded.

Ada explained then that since Jen was out of commission, Miss Irma was going to find someone else to go, but Ada didn't trust Miss Irma's choice of partners, so she asked if she could just do it with me, and Irma said fine.

I guess it's probably not a normal reaction, but I felt weirdly flattered at that. Still, I was kind of nervous. I've heard of this kind of thing before, mostly in locker-room jokes at swim meets, but I wasn't exactly sure what the client would be expecting.

"What will I need to do?" I asked her.

"It's nothing, really," Ada said. "He probably just wants to see us kiss and make out a bit, and then he'll want to get off. I'll take care of that part, and you'll still get half the money. And it will be at my rate, not yours, so a lot more than you got last time." She bit her lip as she looked at me. "I appreciate this so much. But you know you don't have to do it, right? If you're not comfortable."

I put a hand on hers and smiled. "It's okay. I don't mind."

And I didn't. I had been so filled with dread over even just the idea of a phone call, and I was so sure I never wanted to do anything for Miss Irma again, but this was different. Maybe I should have been more freaked out at the idea, but it didn't

86

seem gross or weird as long as it was with Ada. It seemed like fun, almost. Like we were playing a wicked little game. Which I guess we were.

I almost abandoned ship before we even began, though. Just as we got to the door, I felt a weird little rush as the memories of my last time came back to me. I had a vision of that same man coming to the door, or someone like him. I imagined how cold and impersonal it would all be, and my stomach turned and I had a sudden urge to run away, dash toward the fire exit, and run down sixteen flights of stairs just so I could breathe. But right then Ada touched my arm and smiled and I felt better.

She asked me what name I was using, and I realized I still hadn't come up with one. I got nervous that I would completely blank out, like the last two times it came up, so I just said the first name that popped into my head: Justine. It's my French teacher's name, and I don't even know why I said it, but Ada said she liked it, so I guess it's okay.

When the guy opened the door, Ada introduced me as Justine and herself as Brigid. The guy said his name was Marco, but who knows? That might be fake too. He was in his twenties, I'm pretty sure, and he said he worked for a record company. He asked if either of us knew how to sing, and I was worried for a second that he wanted us to sing for him, but he just laughed at the stricken look on my face and took a seat in a little sitting area near the window. Ada and I stayed standing. I wasn't sure what he was expecting. Should we sit on the bed? Take our clothes off? Start kissing? I figured I would follow whatever Ada's lead was, but she was as frozen as I was. She was smiling though. I tried to smile too, but it felt awkward and fake.

Marco grinned back and gestured at the love seat across from him as he pulled a little packet of papers and a bag of something out of his pocket and started rolling a joint. "You guys smoke?" he said.

"No," I answered automatically, but Ada shot a look at me.

"Are you sure?" said Marco. "It helps you relax."

"Go ahead," said Ada. "You should try it."

I looked back at her, trying to figure out what was going on in her head.

"But you said . . . ," I began, remembering our conversation in the car over.

Ada giggled. "That's different," she said. "I was talking about hard drugs. This is legal."

Marco had finished his joint and lit it, inhaling deeply, then taking a long time to exhale the thick smoke. He handed the joint to Ada, and she held it expertly in her fingers, taking a small, delicate drag. She handed it to me.

"Don't inhale too much, or you'll cough," she said. I started to bring it to my lips, but I hesitated at the last second.

"I don't know if—," I began, but Marco interrupted.

"Go on," he said. "Try it. You'll like it."

Ada gave me an encouraging nod, so I brought the joint to my lips once again and pulled. The heavy smoke filled my mouth and throat immediately. I struggled so hard not to cough that my eyes watered. I did let out a little cough/hiccup, but at least I didn't have a huge coughing fit. At first I was mostly aware of the smell and the taste of it, and the harsh burning feeling in my throat, but then I noticed that my head felt a little foggy. But I'm not even sure if that was the pot or just the weirdness of the situation. Honestly, I don't think I inhaled enough to really feel anything.

After a while Marco started fidgeting impatiently, and Ada took the cue to nudge me into a kiss. My mouth was so dry and hot, the wetness of her mouth felt like a relief, and I leaned into it. I had to admit, this was much nicer than anything that happened with that old man. Maybe even nicer than what I did with Damon. I realized right then that I still had never hooked up with anyone I actually knew for more than a few hours. So maybe it's not so surprising that it felt really comfortable and relaxed, like a natural extension of our friendship, instead of this awkward, artificial business arrangement. But that might also just have been the pot.

It wasn't quite how Ada had said it would be. Mostly Marco just watched, but sometimes he came over and put his hands on us, and sometimes he moved us this way or that to position us the way he wanted, as if he were a movie director. And he whispered directions and encouragement too, which was a little strange but not so bad. In a way, I started to see what Ada had been talking about the other day: that it could be fun to know you were giving pleasure to someone, fulfilling their fantasy. It made me feel sort of powerful.

Eventually he moved us to the bed and helped us take off each other's clothes, and then he mostly watched from then on. When he was ready to finish up, Ada took care of him while I just watched. A few times he reached for me, but I just giggled and kissed him a little, and each time Ada did something to distract him.

Ada's really talented. Watching her work was educational, in a way. It made me want to get better, so I could be skilled like her.

By the time they finished, my head was feeling a lot less fuzzy, but I was suddenly starving. Ada giggled when my stomach grumbled as we got dressed. We didn't really say anything until we got down to the lobby. Even though the whole experience had been sort of fun, it felt a little awkward afterward. But just as we were about to go through the big revolving doors, Ada stopped me with a hand on my elbow. I turned to look at her.

"Honey," she said, "are you . . . ? Are you all right? With everything, I mean . . ."

I nodded, and the smile that came to my face was completely unforced. "Yeah," I said. "It was okay. I mean . . . It was kind of fun, actually."

Ada smiled back. "Good," she said. "Hey, he slipped me a tip while you were getting dressed. You want to go get something to eat?"

We wound up at a diner Ada knew, and we both got burgers and fries and milk shakes, and it felt like an indulgence. Ada explained about how the guys tip sometimes, but I should never tell Miss Irma about it, or she'll insist on taking a cut. So that's good to know.

At one point I glanced at my watch and realized I was supposed to be in history class right then, and I couldn't help giggling. I also couldn't stop talking about how great the burgers were, and Ada laughed at me. I was like, "What?" And she said, "Nothing. It's just cute. You've never smoked pot before."

I looked down at my burger. "Oh my God," I said. "Is this what people mean by the munchies?" And we both lost it to giggles.

"But I don't understand," I said when we had recovered a little. "On our way over, you were telling me . . . I mean, didn't you say I should stay away from . . . ?"

"This is different," she said. "Jen was using heroin. This was just pot."

"So pot's okay, but nothing else?"

Ada pressed her lips together. "It's not that simple," she said. "Pot's not such a big deal, and it doesn't really count if it's with a client. Now, if the client offers you drugs and you don't want to do them, you can always say no. But it's more polite to accept. And everything goes a little more smoothly if you do it. But as long as you only do drugs when someone else offers them to you, you can't get into too much trouble."

I nodded slowly, trying to reconcile all this information with what she had told me before in the car. I'm still really new to all of this.

But today wasn't so bad. I'm still not quite sure what I want to do for the future. I need to think about it. Maybe it's one of those things that gets easier with practice, or as you get more used to the feelings and to the different types of clients.

The other thing is, it's nice to have something in common with Ada again. The truth is, when I'm not doing dates and stuff, but just living a normal life, I don't really have anything to say to her. I worry that she'll get bored with me. As long as I keep working like she does, we have this bond.

Sat, Dec 13

I've been thinking a lot about the date the other day with Ada. I had fun, but I also felt kind of like an imposter. I know I'm still very new to all this stuff, but watching Ada work just made me aware of how much I don't know.

It's like when you go to a restaurant and the waitress says, "Hi! Just so you know, it's my first day," and you smile but inwardly you groan because you know she's going to mess up your order or forget about you completely or spill water on your shirt and generally be a big nuisance. That's how I felt. Like there was this whole encyclopedia of stuff I'm supposed to know, and I am pretty clueless about all of it.

I mean, not that I've never heard of a blow job, and on paper it doesn't sound like rocket science. But the mechanics of it are surprisingly . . . It's not easy to get the hang of. Also it's really gross, and I'm not sure how to get over that.

Miss Irma said it was okay to have things you won't do, but blow jobs probably shouldn't be on that list. I'll look like a real idiot if I won't do that, because it's not even that weird. Plus, I'd probably lose a lot of money to the other girls. So I just need to get better at it somehow.

And there are probably a lot of other things clients might ask for that I've never even heard of, so I don't know whether they should be on my list or not. I guess I need to do some research. Thank God for the Internet. . . . I don't even want to think about how girls like me had to figure this stuff out fifty years ago.

Wed, Dec 17

It's payday today! Ada and I are going to leave at lunch to go to Miss Irma's office together and pick up our envelopes. I'm not as scared this time, since I've seen how it goes. I only have to talk to Anne, not Irma. Plus, it will be sooo much better this time because my envelope will have actual money in it! No more start-up fees coming out of my pay. Maybe Ada and I can finally go shopping afterward.

Wed, Dec 17, later

Guess there's been a change of plans. I just got a call from Anne. She told me I'm not supposed to go to the office to pick up my envelope today. I'm supposed to go Saturday. And she gave me a totally different address to go to. I asked if Ada could wait until Saturday too, so we could still go together, but Anne told me that Miss Irma wants to see me alone.

Miss Irma wants to see me? I don't understand. I'm really confused. Why would Miss Irma waste her Saturday handing cash over to a newbie like me? And why at a different address? And why can't Ada be there?

I tried to ask Anne what was going on, but she told me not to worry. That Miss Irma just wants to have a private conversation with me. That doesn't make me worry any less, to be honest. I like Miss Irma so far, and Ada says she treats everyone well, but at the same time, the morning after my night with Damon, Ada seemed scared of Irma. At the very least, she is definitely intimidating. What does she want to talk to me about? Did she find out about Damon? Am I in trouble?

Should I even go? Maybe if I just don't show up and let her keep the money, she'll let it drop. Except I want the money. I mean, I earned it, didn't I? There wasn't much point in showing up to the date if I'm going to chicken out on picking up my payment.

Sat, Dec 20

That was . . . interesting. It wasn't what I was expecting at all, but I have a lot to think about now. I had to take three buses to get to Miss Irma's house, which was in an out-of-the-way suburb. I'd never been there before, but I've heard my parents mention it. A lot of people they knew from Taiwan live around there, though it's a mixed neighborhood.

From the outside the house looked nice but reassuringly normal. Not that different from my house. It has a pretty garden, and I wondered for a moment if Miss Irma works in the garden the same way my mom does. But Miss Irma has a career; she must be too busy for that. She must hire people.

Miss Irma welcomed me at the front door and invited me back to what she called her "office." She was wearing jeans and a pink shirt, which was a little strange, compared to how sharp and businessy she had looked when I met her the other time.

I guess it's not so strange for her to dress down on a Saturday, but it was weird to see her looking so . . . normal. But reassuring, too. I couldn't quite believe she would want to yell at me or fire me or whatever in her weekend clothes.

She told me to take a seat and offered me a glass of lemonade. Then she asked me how I was doing with the work. How I felt about how things were going. I was feeling awkward and not at all sure what she was looking for, so I just said everything was fine. Then she brought up my first client, and I got that feeling in my stomach like in class when the teacher starts handing back the graded exams. I wasn't exactly sure I had passed.

"The client contacted me," she said in that slow, precise way of hers. "He had a few . . ."

"Complaints?" I said, feeling queasy.

"Suggestions."

"I'm sorry," I said quickly, feeling like I was defending myself to my mom after getting yet another bad grade. "I . . . I'm still new to this. There's a lot of stuff I don't know, but I'm trying to learn. And I'm a . . ."

Irma held up her hand, and I closed my mouth, dropping my eyes in embarrassment.

"Don't apologize," she said. "And don't worry. In this business, skill and knowledge can be useful. But another kind of knowledge is even more useful."

I looked up.

"You might have guessed by now," she went on. "Men who are looking for skill don't hire sixteen-year-olds. Your innocence is a selling point. Keep it as long as you can."

"Oh," I said, surprised. "But Ada . . . She's so sophisticated. And talented. Don't men like that?"

"Some men, yes. But you have something Ada will never have. It can make you a lot of money, if you know how to use it."

I couldn't believe that. What could I possibly have that Ada didn't?

"Why do you think men choose you when I show them your picture next to Ada's?"

"I—I have no idea," I answered honestly. It seemed impossible that anyone would do that.

"You want to know what they say? They say, 'I want the Asian girl.'"

I looked up at her, startled.

"They pick me because I'm Asian? But . . . why?"

"Probably because they are racist pigs," Miss Irma replied with a delicate shrug. "But it's not important. What's important is if you keep them happy, they can make you rich. Those pigs have made me very rich."

I fidgeted in my seat, trying to take this information in.

"But if all they care about is my race," I said slowly, "why did that man complain about me?"

Miss Irma leaned forward and steepled her fingers on the desk.

"Try to understand, my dear," she said. "When clients ask for an Asian girl, they are not talking about skin color. Not really. What they want is the fantasy in their head. The fantasy they have been fed. You know this fantasy, because it has been fed to you too. They want a dragon lady. They want a kung-fu princess. They want a Japanese schoolgirl."

"But I'm not Japanese."

Miss Irma cocked an eyebrow at me. "For the right price, you can be Japanese enough." She stood up and stepped out from behind her desk.

"Come with me. I will show you something."

I got up and followed her into another part of the house. She opened a door and I noticed immediately that things were different here. The decor in most of the house was just normal, tasteful suburban, like the houses of most of my classmates. But in this part of the house, it was totally different, like something out of a Chinatown tourist shop or a Hollywood back lot.

Right away I was dazzled by all the red and gold in the room. Once my eyes adjusted to that, I was able to pick out other details: lacquer and jade and porcelain and bamboo. Dragons and peacocks and cranes and Buddhas. It was like a Pier 1 Imports had exploded all over her living room.

"Tell me," said Miss Irma. "What do you notice?"

"I . . . well . . . it's all Asian stuff," I said. "A lot of it reminds me of stuff my mom has lying around, or stuff I've seen when we visit family in Taiwan."

"And the rest?"

I felt a little embarrassed to say what I thought about the other stuff, but a look from Miss Irma reassured me that she wouldn't be offended.

"It looks more like stuff I've seen in some Asian restaurants, I guess," I said. "Kind of a mishmash of different countries and cultures and styles."

"Very good," said Miss Irma. "Perhaps you have guessed that I entertain clients in these rooms." So I had been right that she didn't have the clients visit her in that antiseptic office downtown. "Some of them have known me for a long time. They have certain expectations."

"But it's not real," I said. "It's all stereotypes."

Miss Irma shrugged. "What does it matter? We give them a fantasy, and they give us money. Everyone is happy that way."

She sat down on one of the low, cushioned benches and indicated that I should do the same.

"When I was young," she said, "almost as young as you, I worked in an Oriental massage parlor. It was run by a man, and he made it a very hard life. Not like you girls have now. Others who started with me couldn't take it. They let men abuse them until they were all used up. But I stayed focused. I saved my money. I learned how to keep books, how to keep police away. I studied and used my head. One day all the other girls worked for me.

"You're like me, I think. A smart girl and hardworking. Keep your head, study what the clients want, and give them their fantasy." She leaned forward and patted my knee. "You will do better than the others."

I didn't know how to respond. I admit, I didn't feel totally comfortable with her suggestions. Miss Irma was so different from my mom, but in some ways they were remarkably similar. Always full of directions of how I should act and behave to be pleasing to anyone but myself.

Luckily, Irma didn't seem to expect me to say much of anything. When she had said her bit, she simply handed me a plain white envelope. I was surprised when I saw it and didn't reach for it immediately. Strangely enough, I had almost forgotten why I had come in the first place—not to receive lessons in making myself appealing to men, but to pick up my payment.

I was embarrassed to look through the envelope in front of Irma. It seemed rude, so I let her show me out her front door before I stopped and checked it. And as I flipped through the bills inside, I suddenly felt a lot better about our conversation and my new vocation. Living up to the images my mom and Miss Irma expected felt like being stuck in a cage, but having an envelope full of cash that I earned through my own work . . . that felt like freedom.

Sun, Dec 21

I got a text from Ada today just as I was helping clear the table from lunch. It couldn't have come at a better time. Mom was hassling me again about why she didn't see me working on my homework so much anymore, what's going on with my grades, and why am I so disobedient, blah, blah, blah. I couldn't wait to get out of there, so when Ada texted to see if I wanted to go shopping with her, I texted right back that I would meet her downtown.

Of course Mom the busybody wanted to know who I was talking to and why. Out of instinct, a lie rose to my lips about how it was someone from my English class, and we're working on a group project, and I have to go meet them at the Starbucks a few blocks away. But the words died in my throat. I just thought, *I can't do this anymore. I don't want to do it. I am sick of leading a double life.*

So I just told her. I mean, I didn't say, "It's my hooker friend and she's helping me pick out clothes I can wear while turning tricks." But I did say, "It's a friend. I'm meeting her to go shopping." Which, as far as Mom is concerned, might as well be the same thing. She nearly hit the roof when I said that. It stunned her silent for a second or two at first, and I could read on her face the internal battle she was waging between telling me off for disrespecting her and telling me off for doing something fun with my weekend when my grades were so disappointing. And maybe also joining the battle was the nosy part of her who couldn't bear to imagine I might have a friend she didn't know about.

But that was only a moment or two before she burst forth with her battle cry. The approach she went with was the grades—how I wasn't going anywhere until I had done all my homework and brought my grades up, etc., etc. Which almost made me laugh. As if there was ever really an "until." In my whole life, even when I was doing really well, my grades have never been good enough for me to deserve going off and doing something fun by myself. There would always be another task for me to complete, another thing I'm just not doing quite well enough at.

Well, I'm tired of living in her prison. If she wants me to stick around a minute longer, she's going to have to chain me to the radiator. And until she does that, I will go where I please. Her guilt trips can't affect me anymore.

Sun, Dec 21, later

Back from my shopping trip with Ada. After the scene earlier today, Mom is currently not speaking to me, which is a relief. I bet that won't last, though.

But the shopping trip! It was . . . well, it was definitely fun. But it was also, I don't know . . . I guess I couldn't help being a little disappointed. For so long, my fantasy was that I could become a little more like Ada. She is so beautiful and glamorous and sophisticated, and I've always been so bad at any of that stuff. Just dumpy and geeky and nothing anyone should have any reason to notice. A big part of why I got into this whole lifestyle in the first place was so I could be more like her: gorgeous and mysterious and set apart from all the other girls at school.

I wanted to make money so I could buy clothes and makeup like hers and not have to rely on her hand-me-downs. That was what the money was for. I didn't really have anything else I wanted or needed. But now . . .

After what Irma told me the other day, that's not really an option, is it? She was pretty clear about what the clients would expect from a girl like me. I'm supposed to look cute and young, like a schoolgirl, because that's their fantasy. Well, that's not my fantasy! But since when has anything I wanted ever mattered?

But I suppose if what I wanted was to be noticed, this new look will at least help me accomplish that.

I met up with Ada, and we stopped for coffee first while I told her about what had happened with Miss Irma and I explained to her all about the "look" I was supposed to have now.

Ada nodded and seemed to understand. She talked about it in another way, too. She said that when you think of it as playing a character, sometimes it was easier to get through a date. A bad client couldn't touch you or hurt you the same way if the person on the date wasn't really you. I guess that makes sense. I just wish I got to play a cooler character.

Ada did make me feel better about it. She thought the schoolgirl outfits were cute, and she wished she could get away with them. I don't really believe her, but it was nice of her to say. And she did take me to some stores where I could get stuff that looked better than I was expecting. I've seen the schoolgirls in Taiwan, and believe me, they don't look like anyone's fantasy. The school uniforms are almost as dowdy as my regular school clothes: plaid skirts down to the knee and shapeless white blouses that make everyone look puffy. And knee socks that are always slipping down. The stuff Ada picked out for me was like that, but the sexy version, I guess. The skirt was much shorter, the socks went up higher, and the shirt was a lot more formfitting. I came out of the dressing room feeling a bit shy, and Ada said I looked really cute.

I bought a few outfits along those lines, plus some decent makeup; then we went back to her place to play dress up. I stayed a couple of hours until it started to get dark, and then I got a little nervous about my parents waiting for me at home. I could call them, of course, but I wasn't quite ready to face that conversation yet. Instead, I asked Ada a question I'd wondered about before.

"Why aren't your parents ever home?" I asked her. "Do they work a lot?"

Ada barked out a laugh. "Work? I'm the only person in this household who works."

I didn't know how to respond to that. I just stared at her.

"So they just . . . ," I began.

"There's no 'they,'" she said. "I don't have a father."

"Oh," I said. "Did he die?"

"Beats me," she answered in a hard voice. "Maybe. I don't have the slightest idea who he is, and neither does anyone else, as far as I know."

"What about your mom?"

"She's here. Around. She always is."

"Why haven't I ever seen her?"

Ada shrugged. "She's in her room. Doesn't come out much."

"Oh," I said. "What does she do in there?"

"Mostly lies around in bed." Ada hesitated. It was clear she wasn't used to talking about this. "She's not . . . healthy," she said at last.

"What's wrong with her?"

Ada got up and moved around the room, picking things up at random and putting them back down. She seemed agitated, and I kind of hated myself for bringing up the conversation. It was none of my business. Why had I insisted on prying like my mom would? I was just about to tell Ada that she didn't have to say anything more when she spoke again.

"I don't know," she said. "She wasn't always like this, though she was never what most people would call a normal mom. She used to get . . . episodes, where she would take to her room and not talk and hardly move for days at a time. Then, after a couple of days, she'd snap out of it and put some clothes on and go to the store and get some groceries. Then, one time, she just . . . didn't come out of it."

"She's been like this ever since?"

"Not exactly. Sometimes she gets up and comes out and even tries to make some food. But it's not like before. The truth is, it's better for me when she keeps to herself," she said in a rush of breath. "She's easier to deal with that way."

I nodded as if I understood, though I didn't really. But at least I realized I didn't really want to know any more, and Ada didn't seem to want to give me more details than she already had.

It was getting late anyway, so I told her I had to catch the bus home and I got out of there.

Tues, Dec 23

Now that I have some new clothes, Miss Irma has suggested (via Anne) that I expand my page on the website to include

106

more than just my old head shot from the day I started. It's funny. I didn't even realize Miss Irma had a website. I never thought before about what she did with that photo that Anne took. Now it seems obvious. Who doesn't have a website these days?

Immediately after I found out, I went to look for it online, but I couldn't get into the site. You need a password. The front page is surprisingly discreet, though. It's not like those porn sites that throw up a million pop-ups and start automatically playing a video of a girl and a horse (okay, maybe that was just one site I stumbled on to). You wouldn't have any idea what it was promoting if you didn't already know. There isn't even anyplace for entering your credit-card number. Just a form requesting your username and password but no way to sign up. I wonder how the whole thing works.

I'm honestly not sure about this, though. Do I really want seminaked pictures of myself on the Internet? That seems like the kind of thing people warn you about. Like, what if I want to become a Supreme Court justice or something at some point? Although maybe that ship has already sailed. Maybe once you start having sex for money, all regular ambitions are closed to you.

Still, it does seem like crossing a line of some sort to let someone take pictures. Right now I could stop tomorrow and no one would really know. Miss Irma has my real name, but she seems pretty good at keeping secrets, or else her whole business would fall apart. The clients know me only as Justine, except for Damon. And then there's Ada. As a group, that seems pretty safe. And even if Damon tried to tell someone at some point, he wouldn't have any proof. Just his story. Maybe it's better to keep it that way. . . .

I don't know. I'll ask Ada.

Wed, Dec 24

Last day of the semester today! Tomorrow we'll all go get dim sum in the city, and I'm looking forward to it. We don't really celebrate Christmas, but going into Chinatown is our tradition, since everyplace else is closed that day. We always have a huge meal and see loads of family and friends.

I'm so glad for a break from school! Except, spending 24-7 with my parents isn't much better. Especially since they saw my grades from this semester:

Chemistry: D

American History: C+

Calculus: D

French: B-

English: C

Art: B

Not good. Mom hasn't even really yelled at me—she just cries a lot and won't speak to me. Boy, you'd think I'd murdered someone! I think she's trying to make me feel guilty. Annoyingly, it's working.

I just have to keep reminding myself that I don't care. I don't care about school, and I don't care about my mom's stupid messed-up priorities. If she'd ever taken the time to really get to know me, she wouldn't be so surprised at how I've been acting lately.

At least Mark is home for school break. Now that I don't care about being the perfect daughter, it doesn't bother me so much that he is better than me at everything. It makes me feel a little better, actually. At least my parents have one kid they can't complain about. He's been really good at cheering Mom up, telling her all about his classes and how well he is doing and how all his professors love him.

I hope tomorrow everyone will be able to forget how awful I've been and just have a good time.

Mon, Jan 5

Back to school today. Mark went back to college right after New Year's, which left me climbing the walls with Mom and Dad all weekend. I'm almost glad to have a reason to get away from them.

I wish I had a better reason than school, though. Ada says it's normal that things get quiet with Irma's business over the holidays and that it will pick up again soon. I hope she's right. I need something to think about other than school.

I found out at lunch today that Jenny and Eiko and everyone went to the movies together on New Year's Day and didn't invite me. Not like I care. But still. In a way, we were never very close, but for a long time, they were the only friends I had. I guess they noticed that I've drifted away from them. And maybe also that I'm not exactly keeping up my "nerd" image, what with my last report card.

I wonder if Ada would go to a movie with me.

Wed, Jan 7

I still haven't been scheduled for any new dates. It's annoying, because I spent all that money on the new clothes, thinking I would make it back pretty quickly. But it's hard to make it back when the phone doesn't ring. Maybe I should get those photos done.

I asked Ada about it and she said it's probably a good

idea. She told me more about how the website works, too. Apparently, it's all done by word of mouth. Everyone who signs up with Miss Irma has to come with a reference, and they never even hear of Miss Irma unless someone is willing to vouch for them. Ada says a lot of Miss Irma's clients are famous, and they could have their whole careers ruined if some nosy journalist found out what they were doing. So everything has to be really locked down.

Anyway, she said I would get a lot more dates if I put up a full photo shoot instead of just a head shot. So I said okay, but then Ada was like, just so you know, it will be expensive.

Of course. It hadn't even occurred to me that I would be expected to pay for all this, and of course Anne never mentioned it. But it shouldn't surprise me, after being charged for Irma's phone and the car service. I'm guessing the money for this will come out of my next date. I wonder when I'll ever actually start earning money from this work.

On the other hand, if I don't do it, it looks like I'll never have another date again. And that's no way to make money.

Sat, Jan 10

I had my photo shoot today. It was . . . awkward. And expensive, just like Ada warned me. I really, really hope it was worth it and this brings some more business to me!

I was really nervous about the whole thing, so Ada agreed to come with me for moral support. She helped me pick out some outfits to bring, since I wasn't sure what to expect or what the photographer would have in mind. Plus, I know the site is totally private and Miss Irma is superconcerned with confidentiality, but I still wasn't sure it was entirely a good idea to put seminaked pictures of myself on the Internet. So I went in there looking cute but basically fully dressed, and as I posed for the guy, he kept encouraging me to take this or that off, or hike up a hem or whatever. And every time he did, I would hesitate and resist a bit, then give in.

The guy was good. He made me feel really comfortable and relaxed, so I didn't mind doing it so much, but I was still kind of hesitant. Then Ada came over during a break and was like, "You should really try to speed this up."

"Why?" I said. "Jeb says I don't have to do anything I'm not comfortable with. I'd rather ease into it."

Ada smiled sympathetically and rubbed my arm. "I know," she said. "Jeb is a sweetheart, and he will let you take as long as you need, until you feel completely relaxed. The only thing is, Jeb gets paid by the hour. And he's getting paid by you."

That did put things in a different light. I thought about how I'd act with my clients . . . maybe dragging things out a bit on purpose if I thought I could get another hour's pay out of them. So after that I just bit the bullet and took off almost all my clothes and let Jeb pose me however he wanted. I tried to forget about the camera and my image being plastered all over the Internet.

Now that I look back on it, I'm kind of horrified at some of the pictures I let him take. If my mom ever saw those! I don't even want to think about it. As long as it works, I guess it doesn't really matter.

Thurs, Jan 15

Finally had another date today. I guess those pictures I took are at least doing their job. When I got to the client's room, I did my best to play up the whole Japanese schoolgirl angle, though it was hard to tell if the guy cared at all. He seemed pretty indifferent to everything I did or said. I think he mostly just wanted to pose me like a doll.

It was fine, nothing that crazy or weird, but let's just say that by the end, I was really looking forward to washing my hair. I almost asked if I could use the shower in the hotel room, but I wasn't sure if Miss Irma has a rule about that.

In any case, the guy seemed like he wasn't particularly eager for me to stick around longer than absolutely necessary, so I got out of there.

Made for a gross ride home on the bus though. Luckily, public transit passengers in Seattle are good at minding their own business.

Mon, Jan 19

This date was much better than the last one. The guy was older and kind of smelled weird, but I ended up enjoying my time with him. I think he was mostly lonely and wanted someone to talk to. He told me about his dead wife and about how he has to travel so much for work that hotels feel like home to him. Since he wanted to talk, I asked him to tell me stuff about all the places he'd traveled, and he seemed to enjoy that. I did, too. He had some really funny stories.

The only weird part was afterward, when he got very sentimental and wanted to kiss and cuddle for a while, and then he told me I reminded him of his daughter. Awkward. I'm just glad he didn't mention that at the beginning of the date.

Anyway, I can't really complain because he was a very nice man, and he also gave me a *huge* tip. I'll be honest—that goes a long way to putting me in a good mood. The money itself is nice, and it's also just nice to feel appreciated.

Wed, Jan 21

Another day, another date. This guy was a real creeper, but at least I felt like I was giving him his money's worth with the whole

Asian fantasy. As soon as I introduced myself, he said, "Do you know why I picked you?" I said no and started to undress, while he told me about how he'd been in the military for years, stationed in Okinawa and the Philippines, and how much he missed the whores there. I don't know why, but for some reason that grossed me out. It's weird that people consider me interchangeable with these random people on the other side of the world. But it's not like he knows any of us, so what does it matter?

Still, I hoped that he would shut up once we got down to business, but this one was another talker. He told me all about how he had traveled the world in search of whores who could re-create those experiences, and then he described in great detail what all his previous whores had looked like, including graphic descriptions of certain parts of their anatomy (for which he had a truly amazing memory) and how they compared to my own.

Then, at the end, when I was getting dressed, he said it was a shame he hadn't met me earlier, because he really "prefers them younger," and he grinned and asked me if I had a little sister. Yuck.

Also, no tip.

Mon, Jan 26

I got called into the office today because of all the school I've been missing when I'm off with clients. The assistant principal kept me there for almost an hour, making threats and trying to extort promises to reform. I just kept saying it wouldn't happen again. Easier than trying to fight back. They said they would get in touch with my parents, but what good will that do? It's not like my parents can control what I do or where I go in school.

Funny thing was, the whole time she was browbeating me about missing class, she never once asked me what I was doing in that time.

Fri, Feb 6

Originally I planned to write about every date I go on, but I've skipped a couple because, honestly, there's not that much to say. I guess it's like any job. . . . After a while, you're just going through the motions, and they all seem to blend together.

But the guy yesterday was kind of exciting. My first celebrity! Ada told me we get them from time to time, because everyone knows they can trust Irma to keep their names out of the papers.

I know this is my private journal, but before I went on this date, I got a special phone call from Miss Irma herself reminding me of the importance of confidentiality and how I really couldn't tell anyone. And it's not like writing it in here would be telling anyone, but who knows who might find this journal one day? So I'll just say it was a musician. A pop star, actually. From a boy band! I'll just leave it at that, because if I said anything more, it would become pretty obvious. Luckily, it's not a band I'm actually a fan of, so I didn't have to worry about being too starstruck.

The weird thing is that with a guy like this, you'd think he'd have no trouble getting a date. I mean, anytime it's announced that he's going to be somewhere, girls my age line up for hours and hours just for the possibility of seeing him. Surely a pretty high percentage of those girls would go to bed with him. But I guess I should know by now that it's a myth that guys go to whores only because they can't get it for free. Maybe for some guys, but there are a lot of reasons why people go to prostitutes—confidentiality probably being a big one, in this case.

The plus side of a date like this was that the guy was young (not much older than me, in fact) and really cute. Like, I'd always sort of figured with movie stars and pop stars that they look great in the magazines, thanks to all the airbrushing and stuff, but that in real life they probably look pretty ordinary and you wouldn't even notice them walking down the street. But that was definitely not the case here! I think part of it was him having a very expensive haircut and very carefully chosen clothes and stuff. But there's no question—he was really good-looking. And he had a certain aura about him. Or maybe "magnetism" is a better word. I kind of just couldn't stop looking at him. But I'm not sure if he's famous because he has this quality, or if he has it because I know he's famous.

The minus side was that he was kind of a spoiled little jerk. Like, he could be charming and powerfully compelling when he wanted to be, but the minute he got sick of that act, it was like flipping a switch. Then it was more like babysitting a two-year-old who hasn't had his nap. Draining!

Still, it was kind of exciting, and I didn't mind putting up with it for a few hours. I did feel kind of bad for his regular handlers, who have to deal with him all day, every day. Glad that's not my job.

Sun, Feb 8

I really don't know what I am going to do about my parents. How much longer can we keep up like this?

It's been some time now that I've been basically ignoring them: coming and going as I please and just slamming my bedroom door on all their lectures. I eat most of my meals out, or grab something and bring it back to my room, so it's not too hard to just avoid them.

And for a while it was really liberating. Just not caring what they thought. Doing whatever. I used to cower in fear of them, and now I don't even know what I was afraid of. Did I really think they were going to kick me out of the house or something just for getting a B on a test?

I don't know. Not really. Mom never did anything but yell a little and tell me how to do things better and tell me how disappointed she was. And what a no-good, worthless child I was. That used to hurt me so much! I think I was living my whole life to avoid that feeling of being told I wasn't good enough. But it didn't matter how hard I tried to avoid it, because nothing I did was ever good enough, so I heard it all the time anyway.

But I'm free from all that now. I don't care what they think of me, or how disappointed they are, or what a terrible child I am. And that means they can't hurt me anymore. I go where I want. I come home when I want. I blow off school whenever, and I don't even worry about the school's office calling anymore. What are they going to do to me? I've taken away their power.

Unfortunately, it doesn't work the other way. Just because I've stopped caring doesn't mean my parents have. And I guess it is a little hard to completely turn off my feelings. Mom doesn't yell at me like she used to, but she doesn't ignore me, either. She waits up every night I am late getting home, and anytime she sees me leaving the house in my new clothes, she wrings her hands and her eyes tear up, but she no longer bothers to say anything.

Most days I can shrug this off, but some days it's hard. Some days I just want to bow my head and put on my old clothes and get my books and sit at the kitchen table to study, just so I can see her approving smile again. But, obviously, I can't go back.

Tues, Feb 10

Mom came in my room today as I was taking off my makeup after a date. Out of instinct, my shoulders tensed up, but she didn't yell. She just looked at me silently for a moment and then sat down on the bed. She spoke to me softly in Chinese, asking what happened to me. What have I been doing? I turned to her to say something, but she held up her hand. "No. Don't tell me," she said. "I don't want to know. I think it would break my heart."

She stood up to leave, and just before she closed the door behind her, she turned and said, "What has happened to my little girl?"

I may have cried a little once the door shut. So much for not caring.

It's not fair for her to be nice all of a sudden. What am I supposed to do with this? It's too late. I can't go back to being her good little obedient daughter. Not after the things I've seen and done.

But I can't keep living here like this. School, too. Lately I just can't stand it. Other than Ada, it's so lonely, and since I've pretty much given up caring about my classes, it feels boring and pointless too. Why am I wasting six hours a day there, doing nothing? Wouldn't it make more sense for me to direct my own life?

I wonder what it would take. What if I quit school and moved out? Could I do it? Could I live on my own like a grown-up? Could I make enough money to support myself so I wouldn't have to answer to anyone but myself? Wouldn't have to face anyone's judgmental eyes? That sounds amazing. Now, that would be real freedom. But I would get lonely. . . .

What if Ada were with me? Her life at home with her mom is so different from mine, but it doesn't seem like such a great situation either. Maybe this is what we both need. To get away and be independent. Or be dependent only on each other, without all these expectations and pressures and people needing things from us.

I wonder how much money I would have to save up. How long it would take. Of course, it would mean fewer shopping sprees, but would I rather have a sparkly new belt or a life with Ada on our own, where we could be totally independent?

I think I will do some research on what rent on a decent apartment would be and how much we would need for food and stuff.

Thurs, Feb 12

I'm invited to a party! I don't know if I should really be that excited about it. I mean, it's a work party, which I guess are supposed to be lame, but it's not like work in a typical office.

I'm not sure the last time I went to a real party, but it was probably a kid's birthday party with pizza and cake and pin the tail on the donkey. Sometimes I hear about parties at school . . . real parties with making out and beer, but I only ever hear about those after they take place, on Monday mornings when everyone is dissecting the drama.

I am pretty sure this party won't be anything like those, but I don't know much else. Ada says Miss Irma does this every year around Valentine's Day. She presents it as a fun time for everyone. A way for her to show her love and appreciation for the "talent." But Ada says if it were really a gift, Miss Irma wouldn't invite the clients. Which she does. And the clients bring friends who are interested in becoming new clients, or they show up because they want to pick out their next date in the flesh instead of just using the website.

That makes it sound less like a party and more like dim sum . . . where we're the dumplings being brought around on trays and everyone gets to just grab what they like. Though Ada says that most years it doesn't turn into an all-out orgy. Most years. That's comforting.

Still, I can't help being a little excited about it. Most of all because it's a chance to meet the other girls. Ada mentions them from time to time, but I still haven't met anyone except her, and I want to put faces to names, or maybe even make a new friend or two.

Plus, all things considered, it probably wouldn't kill me to flirt with some of the potential clients. It would be nice to have as many regulars as Ada does and get a bit more cash coming in. Then I could tell Ada about my plan for us to get an apartment together.

Oh, the other thing is that the invitation made it very clear that you wouldn't be served alcohol unless you were over twenty-one. How's that for irony! We're there working as prostitutes, but we're not allowed to drink? Miss Irma says drunk teenagers attract cops like nobody's business, and she can't afford the risk.

But Ada said some of the talent bring flasks of liquor and share it around secretly, so everyone winds up getting kind of drunk anyway.

That does sound kind of fun. I think I like the idea of being included in the secret more than anything else. I never pictured myself as the kind of person who would get passed a flask.

Sat, Feb 14

I'm at Ada's house, prepping for the party! She looks so gorgeous, like a Hollywood screen siren from the 1940s. Her hair is ironed into perfect waves, and she's wearing a black bias-cut dress covered in shimmery beads. I wish I could look like her, or at least dress like her. I thought this party might be a place where I could break out of my persona and look sleek and sophisticated like she always does, but Ada said it would probably be better to stick to a version of my usual style. Some of the clients there will have already seen the pictures on the website, and they'll have an easier time recognizing me if I have the same "look." So I have to somehow pull off "cute," "sweet," and "sexy" all at once, which is actually kind of complicated. I've decided to go with a lot of white and pink and a flower motif, but still showing a lot of skin.

Ada said I looked amazing and kissed me on the cheek, so I guess that will have to do. I wish we got to trade characters for the night, but I guess no one wants that.

I am excited for the party but also a little nervous. I really have no idea what to expect. But Ada says not to worry and that Miss Irma keeps the clients on a pretty tight leash. Officially, there is no touching. That rule isn't enforced strictly, but if someone really starts mauling the girls, Irma is prepared to throw them out, and they know it.

I'm not sure I understand why Irma wouldn't just want to keep the clients happy by whatever means possible. That seems like her usual routine. Ada said Irma has learned from her mistakes. Once upon a time she treated it like a buffet. She had everyone pay a flat fee at the door, and then they could take what they wanted. But she didn't like the results.

"Have you ever seen people at a buffet?" said Ada. "They go crazy. Trying to get every last nickel's worth out of the talent. Plus, it took her ages to get the stains out of the upholstery."

(later)

omg the party was so much fun! except I drank too much and probably [illegible] don't care because I had sooooo much fun. and I met a boy! I mean a boy boy, not a client or whatever. [illegible] he was cute. ugh the room is spinning I better gotto got to go to bed.

Sun, Feb 15

Ugh. Now I know why people don't do this all the time. I feel like my brain went through the dryer or something. Maybe it's even still in there. . . . I'm not at all sure it's in my head. And my stomach might be in there with it, because it is definitely going around in circles.

And even worse than the physical stuff is thinking about how I behaved last night. What got into me? I mean, besides a few shots of whiskey. I want to vomit again just thinking about that.

I bet Miss Irma is so mad at me right now. I bet I was such a horrible embarrassment to her. To everyone. To myself.

Oh my God. I didn't even think about my parents. What must they think of me right now? What do they know? I honestly don't remember coming home last night, and I have no idea if I saw them or not. I am so embarrassed and ashamed even thinking about them seeing me in that state. Presumably they would have murdered me on the spot if they had, and I seem to still be here in my bedroom, so . . . maybe somehow I snuck past them.

I can't worry about that now. I need to start by piecing together what actually happened last night. My first clue is the previous entry, which I don't remember writing and I can barely read. That's kind of funny, actually, though also a little disturbing. Wait. Did I smoke pot again last night too? I seem to vaguely remember that. That probably didn't help matters.

All right. Let's start at the beginning.

The party was at Miss Irma's house, in those back rooms where Miss Irma had taken me the last time. She had added some holiday decorations here and there, but not that much, since the rooms were so ornate already.

At first I was really nervous and uncomfortable and kind of clung to Ada. Then I realized I was probably annoying her, so I tried to hide out behind one of the big screens. Ada found me after a bit and laughed. She said as the night wore on, it would be a bad idea to sneak behind the screens, since other people would have that idea too. And from the way she said it, I got the sense that she didn't mean they were shy like me.

Anne came over after a minute and took our coats and pointed out the bar and stuff, with a reminder that we wouldn't be served anything but soft drinks, so not to bother asking. Then she told us to make ourselves comfortable, because the clients would be arriving soon. I was confused by that, because there already were a few guys milling around the room, though they were younger and more attractive than the clients usually were. I thought maybe Irma was hiding a bunch of cute clients like Damon and fixing them up only with the more experienced girls.

Ada offered to show me around and introduce me to everyone, but it was too overwhelming. I felt really bad for holding her back and tried to put on a brave face, but she seemed to get it intuitively. Instead of bringing me over to the big gossiping groups exchanging greetings, she found a spot on a bench in a dark corner and tugged me down next to her.

"How about I give you all the dirt on everyone first?" she said in a whisper. "That way you'll already know who everyone is when you actually meet them."

I almost sighed with relief, and Ada started to point people out and tell me their names and their life stories. I have to admit that some combination of awe and anxiety prevented me from absorbing everyone's names, but almost everyone there had some pretty rough story in their past—violence or molestation or drugs or homelessness. They all seemed happy and okay now, but none of them were like me, with two parents who had plenty of money and didn't hurt them or abuse them. It made me feel sort of bad, like I had wandered into the wrong party. Is there something wrong with me that I took to this life without any trauma pushing me into it?

I did notice when Ada pointed out Jen, since she had mentioned her before. The one with the drug problem. Ada said that both her parents had died when she was little, and she wound up living with a distant relative who beat her, so she ran away and lived on the streets for a while, eating out of garbage cans. It was hard to believe that the person laughing and chatting right in front of me, wearing a designer dress and scarfing miniature quiches, could once have been so desperate. It gave me a newfound respect for Miss Irma, that she offered people like Jen and so many of the others a second chance at life.

Jen's roommate, Beth, was there too. Ada doesn't like her much. I guess there's some history there, but I didn't get the whole story. At some point I asked Ada about the guys who were at the party and who were they if not clients. She laughed.

"They're talent. I can introduce you to them, if you like."

"Wait," I said, resisting her attempt to tug me up by the hand. "What do you mean, talent? What kind of . . . ?"

Ada gave me a funny look. "They work for Miss Irma," she explained. "Just like us." I must have still look confused, because she laughed again, then leaned a little closer to me. "They have sex with men for money," she said slowly and clearly, like she was explaining it to a little kid.

"Oh," I said, trying not to look shocked. I don't know why I was so shocked, though. Why should it be so surprising that boys make money from this just like girls do? Now that I think about it, it seems like the most obvious thing in the world.

I couldn't help staring at this one boy who was standing in a group of girls and talking very animatedly. He was one of the most gorgeous guys I had ever seen, with dark skin and almond eyes and a delicate, heart-shaped face. He was wearing eyeliner and maybe even mascara, but I could tell that even without that he would be almost as pretty as any girl I had ever seen. I asked Ada about him, and she said his name was Shawn. She didn't tell me much about him, but I got the sense she didn't like him very much.

At that point there was a noise and the din in the room died down. Miss Irma was standing near the bar, tapping a glass for everyone's attention. I almost didn't recognize her in a flowing peacock-blue kimono. She had a drink in one hand and her phone in the other.

"Thank you for your attention," she said in her carefully clipped tone. "The clients will arrive in a minute or two. Some advice, if I may. Do not crowd them like a batch of hyenas. There will be plenty to go around. But do not spend the evening talking to one another as if this were a high school dance, either. Enjoy yourselves, but remember: The clients are our guests tonight. And last, alcohol is strictly forbidden to you, even if offered by a client. Is that understood?"

While she was talking, I leaned over and asked Ada about some men I hadn't noticed before in the room. Not ones like Shawn, but others that didn't seem like clients either.

"That's Miss Irma's security," said Ada. "'Goons' is a better word. She'll act like they're here to protect us in case any of the clients try to take something they haven't paid for, but don't kid yourself. They work for her, not for us. And if she has a problem with any of us, they won't hesitate to toss us out, or worse."

"Worse?"

Ada gave me a significant look but didn't elaborate.

A few minutes later, the clients started showing up. Just as Miss Irma had suggested, it was a little hard to resist the urge to surge toward them, especially when I saw other people doing just that. It was hard not to feel like the first people out of the gate were "winners" in some sense, but I held back. It made sense to wait until there were more in the room so you could actually take your time and pick one who seemed appealing. But then, even when there were more, it kept happening that every time I spotted someone who looked like a good bet, I'd try to catch his eye from across the room only to notice some other girl sidling up to him and running a finger down his arm. Obviously, I needed to be a bit more aggressive.

I did manage to give my cell phone number to a couple of guys, but they didn't seem all that interested. I wondered if my cutesy Asian girl getup had been a bad idea. Maybe it was too niche, and I would have been better off dressing more normal sexy like the other girls.

One guy did grab me as I walked toward the bar and pulled me down onto his lap, but he was pretty gross. He smelled awful and had a lot of hair on his knuckles. I was as pleasant with him as I could manage, and I did give him my number when he asked, but I was already thinking that if he contacted me, I would definitely pretend to be busy that day.

Eventually he let me up and I headed toward the bar, just hoping for a few moments of calm. I got a ginger ale and sipped it slowly, only gradually becoming aware that there was a man leaning against a bookshelf near me, sipping his drink and eyeing the room but not yet talking to anyone. He wasn't exactly good-looking—with a weak chin and a lazy eye—but he seemed pleasant enough and a much better option than most of the other men in the room. I took a deep breath and sidled up to him, running a hand down his arm as I introduced myself, just as I'd seen the other kids do. It didn't seem to work so well, though. He sort of twitched and shifted back a little.

"Nervous?" I said in what I hoped was a flirtatious tone.

He gave me an apologetic smile. "Maybe," he said. "I've never been to a party like this before."

I tried to think of something flirty and suggestive to say, but I drew a blank, so I wound up saying, "Neither have I." Surprisingly, this wasn't such a bad move, since it did give us something to talk about. Though that was awkward too. He kept starting in with questions like, "How did you get into this business?" but then cutting himself off as if maybe he didn't want to know. Still, it wasn't a bad conversation and I was proud of myself for holding up my end and not letting it descend into horrifying awkwardness.

The only problem was, I didn't seem to be making much progress with him. He still startled at all my little touches and still backed farther away every time I moved closer to him, until it looked as though he was trying to squeeze himself into the bookshelf.

I was starting to feel a little bad about it when I noticed someone standing at my elbow.

"Introduce me," said a voice near my ear. I turned and saw Shawn, the pretty boy I'd noticed earlier.

"What?" I said, caught off guard.

Shawn smiled at the client, then leaned in to me. "Introduce me," he said again.

"Oh," I said, and I made the introductions, feeling slightly annoyed that Shawn was distracting me from my awkward attempts to get this guy interested. That's when I noticed the guy's face. He was looking at Shawn with an intensity that I hadn't seen during our whole conversation. And when Shawn laid a hand on the man's forearm, he gave a slight shiver and leaned into it.

Ada's patient explanations popped back into my head. *Oh,* I thought. *Ohhhh.* Shawn gave me a quick grin, which I returned before coming up with some excuse to leave the two of them alone together.

I wasn't sure what to do with myself after that. I glanced around the room, but everyone appeared to be engrossed in conversations. I couldn't see any clients standing alone. Before long, though, I felt a hand at my waist. At first I thought it must be a client, but the cloud of expensive perfume gave Miss Irma away.

She whispered in my ear.

"Come," she said. "No prizes for standing about. You have to talk to people." I started to protest that there was no one to talk to, but she ignored me as her hand guided me toward an adjacent room I hadn't been in yet. A man standing alone was calmly surveying the snack table with his back to the room.

"Damon," said Miss Irma, "where have you been hiding? I want to introduce someone to you."

I don't know why it didn't occur to me that he would be there, but I couldn't have been more surprised. My brain froze in that moment, torn between trying to figure out an appropriate reaction to being suddenly confronted with the man I lost my virginity to and haven't seen since and the flaring memory of Ada reminding me that Miss Irma must never learn what happened between us. I stared up at him and said nothing.

He looked down at me, surprised but not half as dumbstruck as I was. "Oh," he said. "Yeah, we've met."

I felt more than saw Miss Irma's eyes narrow next to me as she processed this information. "You've met? But I don't remember . . ."

"It wasn't through . . . ," I said quickly.

"No," he agreed. "It was . . ."

But neither of us had a very good end to our sentences.

"I see," said Miss Irma, though she still sounded confused and, to my horror, more than a little suspicious. Luckily, I was saved from trying to dig myself out of this hole by Ada, who shrieked from across the room and then barreled toward our little group at full speed.

"Damon!" she cried, launching herself into his arms.

"Ada," he said with a laugh as she burrowed into his chest and squeezed him in a mighty hug. He kissed her forehead and mussed her hair a little. "Long time no see. What've you been up to, kiddo?"

A glance over at Irma revealed a bemused and not entirely pleased expression, but I didn't stick around to see how it played out. I took the opportunity of her distraction to get myself out of there.

That left me wandering the room with nothing to do again, and I was feeling awkward and sort of watching Ada out of the corner of my eye with a weird feeling as she talked with Damon. I don't know why. It's true that I had slept with Damon, but Ada had known him much longer and more intimately than I had, and I had hardly thought of him since that night. I'm not sure why seeing them together bothered me so much. In any case, I didn't have much time to consider the question because I was startled by a touch on my elbow. I tensed up, thinking it was probably Miss Irma about to lecture me again for not flirting with enough guys, but it was Shawn.

"Hey," he said gently. "I'm sorry about earlier. I hope you didn't mind that I jumped in on your conversation."

"Don't be silly," I said. "Obviously I was wasting my time with him." I looked down at my shoes, suddenly abashed. "Mostly I'm just a little embarrassed that I couldn't tell after talking to him for fifteen minutes, while you spotted it from across the room."

Shawn shrugged lightly. "It's kind of a sixth sense. You pick it up with experience. Hey," he said. "Keep an eye out for Miss Irma for a second, will you?"

I was confused, but I checked around for her. She seemed to be in the other room, so Shawn brought a silver flask up to his lips and took a swig, then pressed the flask toward me wordlessly, raising his eyebrows as if in offer. I was nervous, but I couldn't help a little thrilled shiver from going up my spine. Here I was, at a party, and someone was offering me a sip from their flask! As if he really believed I was one of the cool kids.

I giggled a little and took it from him.

"I'll keep an eye out for the Dragon Lady," said Shawn, "but try to keep your head down just in case. Don't draw attention to it."

I nodded and unscrewed the cap, but it's harder than you might think to keep your head down while at the same time tipping it back so liquid can slide down into your mouth. Plus, since the bottle was opaque, I couldn't really judge how much was in it, so it was really hard to figure out the best angle. I did my best, but wound up misjudging and sent a big mouthful of the stuff right down my throat. I was prepared for it not to taste too good, but the burning sensation it left in my throat took me by surprise. I tried to choke it back, but it was too late. . . . I choked and coughed and the stuff came right back up and all over Shawn's shirt.

I don't know if I've ever been more embarrassed in my entire life. This is why I can't have nice things! Because I spit up on them. So basically I wanted to die and was so close to just bolting for the nearest exit or screen or potted plant, but Shawn was really nice about it. He just laughed and said, "Guess you're not too experienced with whiskey, either." I blushed really hard at that, because I get tired of always being the innocent one, but he just rubbed my lower back gently, which made me feel a lot better, and said that it reminded him of his first time drinking whiskey.

He told me he was small as a kid, bullied by older boys, and didn't get any respect. He noticed that the older kids drank alcohol, and he thought if he did too, it would make him seem tough and cool and he wouldn't get picked on anymore. Well, there was this guy, a neighbor and an old friend of the family, who used to have him over all the time when his mom wasn't home, like, to babysit him. They played video games together, talked about school and stuff.

Then one day, the guy offered him some whiskey, so he took a small sip and it almost made him gag. The guy offered him more, and Shawn didn't want to seem like a wimp, so he kept accepting it. At first he tried to take really small sips, but even that made his eyes water. So finally he just took a swig and held it in his mouth, looking for an opportunity to spit it out. The guy kept offering him more, so he took a couple more swigs. Then the guy snuggled up and tried to kiss him, and Shawn spat whiskey all over him.

Shawn laughed at this point. "The dude was so pissed," he said. "I felt like an idiot."

I couldn't help laughing too, even though, now that I think about it, that's a pretty horrible story. But I guess, based on what Ada was telling me earlier in the night, pretty much everyone has a story like that. Maybe it's not such a big deal. I don't know. I always feel so sheltered around these people! Like I don't know a thing about the world. But then I think about all my old friends sitting around the geek table, and most of what they know of the world was compiled from newspaper articles in preparation for debate-team meets. I guess maybe it's not so bad to occupy the middle ground.

Shawn offered me another swig of whiskey, but I really

didn't even want to try it again. I could still feel that awful burning in my throat. Shawn noticed my cup of ginger ale on the table behind me and he said, "Here, try it this way. You'll like it better." And he poured some in. I was nervous to try it again, but it did taste better with the pop. I could still feel the burning in my throat a little, but it didn't instantly make me want to gag. And the flavor on my tongue wasn't bad at all. The whiskey cut the sweetness of the pop in a good way.

"Better?" he said.

I giggled and smiled. "Much better."

"I'm glad we met," he said. I realized that his hand was still on the small of my back. "You're a cool kid—you know that?"

I couldn't help grinning. No, I hadn't known that. Cool kid was about the last way I ever would have described myself. But there I was, sipping whiskey at a fancy party and talking to the prettiest boy there, and I thought, *Maybe he's right. Maybe I am a cool kid.*

I took another sip of the whiskey.

"Did you swallow it?" said Shawn. "Or are you just storing it up in your mouth?"

I let out a giggle.

"No," I said. "I swallowed it."

"Good," he said. He cast a quick glance around the room, clearly scouting for Miss Irma or her goons, but when he didn't spot them, he leaned in closer and he kissed me!

Honestly, I was so surprised I didn't know what to do. I just froze up completely, which is pretty embarrassing given that kissing people is one of the things I do for a living. I can only imagine that he was wondering how I make any money at all at this gig, given how I reacted. But it was different! Different because he is cute. Different because I like him. Different because I wasn't expecting it. But maybe most of all different because . . . Well, let's just say that I was confused.

As my senses started to come back to me, I pulled back. Shawn let me go, and he looked pretty embarrassed.

"I'm sorry," he said. "I didn't mean to—"

"No!" I interrupted. "It's not that. You didn't . . ." We were both babbling pretty stupidly at this point. I stopped and took a deep breath. "It's just that I, well, I thought you were . . . I mean, aren't you . . . ?"

"Gay?" he supplied.

"Well, yeah. I mean, back there, with that guy . . . And Ada said . . ."

Shawn grinned. "Haven't you ever heard of 'gay for pay'?"

"What?" I said. I hadn't. "What do you mean?"

"I mean, it's a job. It's not who I am. Do you fall in love with all the men you date for this job?"

I made a face. "Definitely not."

"Are you attracted to all of them?"

"Hardly any."

Shawn shrugged. "Same for me. And these clothes you're wearing . . . Is this how you dress in your normal life?"

I laughed. "No. I only dress this way because Miss Irma told me to."

"Because the Japanese schoolgirl thing is what the clients want, right?"

I nodded.

"I bet you're not even Japanese."

"Nope."

"So you understand, then. This stuff isn't who I am." Shawn grinned. "When I'm with a guy, I just close my eyes and think about how much money I'm making."

"So you never enjoy any of it at all, then?" I asked. "You've never gotten any pleasure whatsoever from a date?"

Shawn sipped his whiskey. This line of questioning seemed to make him uneasy.

"I enjoy it exactly as much as I need to," he said at last. "For the client."

I was about to apologize for asking a kind of rude and nosy question when Shawn noticed something behind my left shoulder.

"Shit," he said. "The Dragon Lady is on the prowl. She'll

be pissed if she sees us flirting with each other instead of the clients." He gave me a mischievous smile and tugged at my elbow. "Come with me."

He pulled me toward the edge of the room, then slid open a glass door that opened onto a pretty garden and patio. A small group of kids were already clustered around on the patio furniture, talking quietly and trying to muffle their giggles. Shawn slid the door shut behind us. It was chilly outside in the night air but not too bad. Especially since once I shivered, Shawn wrapped his arms around me and squeezed. Then I felt a lot warmer.

"Come on," he said, nudging me toward where the other kids were assembled. I wished I'd remembered Ada's introductions better, but I couldn't remember who was who, and it was hard to even make out people's faces in the darkness. The only people I was sure of were Jen and her roommate, Beth.

Shawn nodded to the crowd like he knew them all, then found a seat on a bench near them and pulled me down onto his lap. I noticed they were passing a couple more flasks around, and some of them were smoking pot out of a little pipe, too. Everyone was quiet except for one girl, who seemed to be wrapping up a story she was telling. I couldn't figure out what had happened, exactly, but it was clear she was describing a very bad date. When she was done, a boy immediately jumped in and started telling a story he described as "his worst date ever." It was really bad! He got into a car with a guy and the guy took him out of the city so he had no idea where he was; then the guy wasn't happy with the sex, I guess, so he . . . well, raped him with a beer bottle. Then he left him in the middle of the woods somewhere. And he didn't even pay him! The kid had to walk all the way into the city while in a lot of pain before he could get a cell signal.

Then another boy jumped in with his worst-date story, about how he showed up at what seemed like a perfectly normal date with a client he knew well, but this time the client had invited a whole bunch of other men without asking, and they were all drunk and rowdy and got violent, and there was nothing he could do.

Then a couple of girls told their worst-date stories. Eventually they started to run together in my mind, maybe because of the effects of the whiskey. Not getting paid or paid enough was a common complaint, and being forced to do things that they explicitly said were off the table. Plus, clients getting violent or unpredictable, or treating them like disposable objects. It should have all been really scary and depressing, but it was hard to get too upset with the whiskey warming my belly and Shawn's arms around my waist. And everyone was sort of laughing and telling these stories like they were funny anecdotes rather than horrifying personal experiences. A big part of me felt terrible for them, and grateful that nothing that bad had ever happened to me. But another, smaller part felt a little . . . maybe jealous isn't the right word. But in some small way, I wished I had a story of my own to contribute, if only so I could feel more like part of the gang. There was something really comforting about that sense of shared camaraderie. I almost felt like people were sharing their worst stories to make each other feel better about what had happened to them. Like if they all went through it together, or if there was always someone who had it worse and survived, then it must not be all that bad.

Eventually, someone told a story that was particularly horrifying because it was her worst time, and it was also her first time. Not losing her virginity, but her first time having sex for money. I couldn't believe she'd actually continued with this profession after what had happened to her (let's just say it involved box cutters; I don't really want to think about it beyond that), but I guess, from the way she told it, she didn't have a lot of options.

But that was good in a way, because people shifted from telling worst-time stories to first-time stories. Maybe everyone in the group realized that after that one, we needed a change of mood. Something a little less grim. Not that the first-time stories were all rainbows and sunshine. There was still a lot of stuff that made me cringe. But it was more in the spirit of laughing together than staring in silent horror.

I was starting to feel pretty drunk at that point, but I happened to notice Ada and Damon slipping outside together. I hoped they would come over and join us, but instead they made their way to a bench at the other end of the garden and sat there talking quietly together. Occasionally, one of Ada's delicate bell-like giggles drifted through the chill night air over to me. I felt bad for my earlier flare of jealousy. Ada's life is hard. She doesn't get a lot of chances to just be happy and content. I was glad that she was enjoying the evening, even if Irma was undoubtedly pissed.

I had lost track of the conversation while watching them, but at some point Shawn squeezed me gently and said, "What about you? I bet you have a good first-time story."

"Oh," I said, blushing. "Well, yes. It was good, but not very interesting, I guess. He took me to the restaurant on top of the Space Needle. It was incredibly romantic, and I had a really wonderful time." I looked down, feeling almost guilty for having had such a good experience, compared to everyone else.

One of the girls laughed. "Was he at least gross-looking? Tell me he was really ugly."

I giggled. "You can judge for yourself," I said. "He's right over there."

Everyone turned to follow my gaze.

"Damon?" said Jen's roommate, Beth. "Your first time was with Damon?" She sounded incredulous.

That's when I remembered I wasn't supposed to tell anyone what happened with Damon. I clapped my hands over my mouth. "Oh my God," I said. "I wasn't supposed to tell anyone that. It was a secret."

"A secret?" repeated Beth. "Why would it be a secret?"

"I don't really know," I explained. "Ada just said I shouldn't tell anyone. Although I guess she didn't mean you guys. It's really just Miss Irma who isn't supposed to know."

"Miss Irma? Why not?"

I was really feeling the whiskey in my veins now. I was having trouble focusing on the conversation and my memories of Damon and what Ada had said about not telling anyone and the feeling of Shawn beneath me and around me. I felt confused. I shook my head, trying to clear my thoughts.

"I'm not sure. Ada just said she'd get in trouble if Miss Irma knew. I shouldn't have said anything. But you guys won't tell, will you?"

Everyone laughed a bit at that, which I didn't understand. One of the boys said, "Believe me. I don't think any of us is so loyal to Miss Irma that we're going to rat each other out to her. There's no good that can come of that. We're much better off standing together."

I nodded, feeling incredibly grateful.

"That's right," I said, remembering Ada's words. "We need to look out for each other."

Just then I caught the distinctive smell of expensive perfume carried toward me on the cold night air.

"What are you doing out here?" came a familiar voice. A voice with a very distinctive Chinese accent.

Everyone got really quiet, and I could almost feel my neighbors sitting up straighter. I kept replaying the conversation in my head, trying to figure out what Irma could have heard.

"Do you think I throw a party every year so you have a chance to talk together?" she went on. "If you want that kind of party, you can throw it yourselves. Right now this is not fun times. You are on the clock, and your job here is to make as many men want you as possible." She paused, but no one moved. "I'm not saying this just for me," she said. "The harder you work, the more we all benefit. Go on, now." She motioned toward the sliding door. "Get back inside and get to work."

A chorus of quiet, shame-faced "Yes, Miss Irma's" came from the group as people got to their feet and headed back toward the door. I stood up, feeling a little unsteady, and as Shawn stood up behind me, I stumbled forward and my feet went out from under me. I tumbled in a heap on the hard concrete of the patio, but it didn't hurt all that much. I said,

"Ow," anyway. Then, as I realized how ridiculous I must look, I started laughing.

Miss Irma froze and stared down at me. "What's going on here?" she said softly, her voice laced with danger. No one said anything, though I noticed a few people making their way quietly toward the door.

"Stand up," said Miss Irma severely. I managed to get to my feet, but the ground seemed to be swaying. I steadied myself on the patio table next to me. Miss Irma leaned in very close to me, looking up into my face. Then she sniffed. "Just as I suspected," she said. "You reek of liquor." She turned to face the others who remained. "And what about the rest of you? What have you been up to out here?"

No one answered.

"Idiots," muttered Miss Irma. "I give you so much, and this is how you repay me. You want us all to be out of a job, I suppose? You would prefer to go back to living on the streets, sleeping in Dumpsters, giving blow jobs for food? Is that what you want?"

Still no one answered, but they shuffled guiltily.

Miss Irma grabbed me by the arm and shook me. "Can you walk? Do you need a hospital?"

My head was still swimming a bit, but I didn't feel that bad. I was just upset that she was yelling at me. "I'm okay," I said quietly.

"I bet," she said. "Fine. Where's your little friend? Ada." She looked around behind her. "Ada!" she called out sharply.

"I'm right here," said Ada, and I had never been so glad to hear her soft, low voice.

"Can you get her home?"

Ada nodded.

"And have you been drinking?"

"No, Miss Irma."

"You are sure?"

"I haven't had anything to drink."

Miss Irma gave her a long sniff. "Fine," she said. "She's your responsibility. Take her home, and if there is any further trouble, you will all answer to me."

After that point, I can put together only bits and pieces. Flashes of me and Ada in a taxi, and trying to find my keys, and then next thing I knew I was waking up in bed and feeling like something you scrape off the bottom of your shoe.

Sun, Feb 15, later

Today has been so awful. Physically I feel a bit better than I did this morning (though still not 100 percent), but emotionally, mentally, I feel completely drained.

When I woke up this morning, based on what I remembered of the night before, I had some little hope that maybe I'd managed to sneak in and get to bed without my parents ever noticing. That was a nice fantasy while it lasted. I guess I temporarily forgot who my parents are. I learned exactly how wrong I was when I got dressed and went downstairs to dig up some breakfast. Mom and Dad were waiting for me, and the minute I saw their faces, I almost turned around and went right back up to my room. The way I was feeling, all I wanted was to drink a huge glass of water and maybe make myself some hot food. The last thing I wanted to deal with was getting yelled at in Chinese.

The weird thing is, they didn't really yell. I guess we're past that now. They didn't even act all that disappointed, like Mom did during our last big conversation. Mostly they just seemed worried. Concerned. Which was even worse. I used to feel guilty every time I did the slightest thing wrong, and I hated that feeling, but it's nothing compared to the guilty feelings I had today.

I sat across from them, starving and parched and feeling trembly and weak, and let the Chinese wash over me, exerting just enough energy to understand what exactly they were worried about. Of course their first question was the obvious: Where were you last night?

So I told them, accurately, if not completely, that I was at a party.

Then they wanted to know if there was alcohol at the party. I guess my drunken state when I got home was less obvious to them than it was to Miss Irma. But then, they have less experience with that type of thing.

Lying seemed pointless, so I told them yes.

They were quiet for a little while. Then my dad said, "Since when do you go to those kinds of parties where there are kegs and no parents?"

I knew it was rhetorical, and my role at this point was just to sit there and look sorry for the shame I had brought on our household, but I couldn't help almost laughing a little, if only internally. It just occurred to me at that moment that my parents were picturing me at a normal high school party. The kind of party that normal high school kids get into normal amounts of trouble for. How would they know any different?

I didn't say anything, but I couldn't help thinking, *If only you knew. It's so much worse than you are even thinking, and you are already so upset.*

Once they had said their piece, I finally got some food and started to feel a little better, so I was going to go back up to my room on the pretense of "doing homework" and take a nice long nap, but Mom and Dad had other ideas. I guess they had been talking while I ate, because afterward they cornered me and had a whole new plan in mind. I don't recall all the details, but I know it involved me never leaving the house again for pretty much anything but school. No extracurriculars, no meetings, and definitely no going out with friends.

And since they can't trust me anymore to tell them the truth about my life, Dad says he's going to meet with all my teachers on Monday to find out what my assignments are, and we'll go over my progress on them all every night. Oh, and I almost forgot the best part—if I don't obey these new restrictions, they're going to send me to Taiwan to live with my grandmother and my aunts!

No way. There's just . . . no way. I can't let that happen. I don't know anyone in Taiwan except a couple of family members, and I barely know the language. It would be just like prison.

And what about Ada? I can't just abandon her. I finally made a real friend. Someone who cares about me, and I care about her. Not just someone who tolerates me sitting with them at lunch or is willing to do group work with me in class. I know Ada acts tough, and she's pretty street-smart, but she is so alone in the world. She needs someone looking out for her.

I have to get away from here. Now.

Sun, Feb 15, later

I've calmed down a bit now. After my last entry I started throwing clothes into a suitcase so I could run away, but as I went through my stuff, I started to think over all the things they had said. I get so frustrated with how they try to control me, and I wish they would just relax and let me make my own decisions about my life, but I guess I have to ask myself if I'm making good decisions.

It's easy to be brave in theory, but some of the stories people told at the party should probably worry me more than they did. What will I do if some client wants to hurt me? If someone wants me to do drugs that leave me confused and not sure how to react? The drinking last night made me realize how out of control you can be when altered by chemicals. In a situation like that, I might not make the same decisions I would make when sober.

Do I have a plan for those circumstances? When I started, Irma said that safety always comes first, and if a situation seemed dangerous, I should leave. But what if I couldn't leave? If I called Anne or Irma or Ada, would they come rescue me? Would they come in time? What if I called the police? Irma wouldn't want that, but should I care? These are difficult questions, and I'm only just realizing I haven't thought them through completely.

I don't know. Maybe I really should just quit. Going back to my old life sounds pretty unappealing, but it's not forever. Once I graduate from high school, I can be on my own if I want. And even if I don't wind up going to college, a high school degree will at least give me a shot at a regular job that wouldn't be so dangerous.

But what about Ada? I can't just walk away from her. And as long as I follow my parents' rules, there will be no room for her in my life.

I guess there's really only one thing that makes sense: I have to keep working for Miss Irma. At least until I can save up enough money for me and Ada to rent an apartment together, like Beth and Jen have. I did some research on it, and I'm pretty close already. It won't take me long to earn that much, plus a bit extra for some security. Then, once we get on our feet, Ada and I can start looking for other kinds of work. I mean, yeah, we'd have to work long hours to make enough money, but normal people do it, so it must be possible. Somehow we'll make it work.

I love my parents, and I don't want to hurt them. But for now Ada needs me more. I just have to make sure I toe their line closely enough so they don't ship me off to Taiwan before I can put this plan into action.

Wed, Feb 18

My date yesterday got a little out of control. According to Anne, it was just supposed to be a normal, straightforward date. Easy peasy, no special requests. But when I got there, the client had lines of what I think was cocaine laid out, and he wanted me to do it with him.

I froze, just running through everything Ada had told me and trying to figure out what I should do. *Stay away from drugs so you don't wind up like Jen,* except I just saw Jen at that party and she seemed okay. *Some drugs are really bad, but others are basically okay, like pot and alcohol.* Which kind was cocaine? I was pretty sure it was a bad one, but then Ada had mentioned doing it a few times, so how bad could it be? Ada said it was always okay to say no, if you didn't want to do it, and I remembered how awful I felt after just a bit of whiskey and pot at the Valentine's party and how out of control they had made me feel. I really didn't want to put myself in that position with a client. But then, Miss Irma would say it's important to keep the client happy. And Ada had said they consider it rude if you say no.

The client was giving me a weird look at this point, and I realized I'd been standing there for way too long. He offered his straw to me again, and finally I decided I'd split the difference and just do a little bit, for politeness' sake.

It was a really weird feeling. The whole concept of sniffing something other than air into my nose was hard to get over, and it took me a couple of tries to even figure out the mechanics of it. Then, once I got it to work, I suddenly felt like I had a cold. My nose got all weird and congested, and there was this really wretched taste in my throat, hard and bitter like a chewed-up aspirin. Why do drugs taste so bad? But I guess that's not why people do them.

To tell the truth, I didn't really feel that much. Like, I didn't feel different the way I did with pot and alcohol. I did notice that I was talking a lot, when normally I talk the very bare minimum in these situations.

But that wasn't really a big deal. The problem was that the guy was taking forever. Technically, it's supposed to be an hour, and in the past I've had some clients go over a bit and I never said anything because I didn't care enough to make a stink about it. But these days I really need to make sure I'm home by the end of the school day, because I know that if I mess up even a little bit, my parents are prepared to ship me off to Taiwan. And I can't let that happen.

So I kept trying to hurry things along, but this guy just kept going. I wasn't sure exactly how much time had passed because I couldn't reach my phone, and from my angle I couldn't see the room's alarm clock. It started to feel like it had been a really long time, though, and I just wanted him to finish. But you can't exactly tell people to hurry up in this line of work—that would ruin the fantasy.

So I tried to suggest a different position, trying to make it sound like a sexy idea rather than a desperate attempt to speed things up, and he was just like, "No, this is the only position that works," and I could tell he was getting frustrated too. So I was trying to be encouraging, and then he says, "It's this fucking condom. I'll never be able to come with a rubber. I need to take it off." And I'm like . . . what? I didn't even know what to say. Condoms are required, obviously, Miss Irma tells all the clients that. Did he think I was insane?

Finally he got off me and I got off the bed and started to get dressed. I'd had enough of him. I just wanted to leave, but that pissed him off. First he couldn't believe it, and he tried to convince me to come back to bed. When that didn't work, he started yelling. "Fuck you, you fucking whore," and all that. And it's not like I've never been called a whore before, and it's not like it's inaccurate, but something about the way he said it upset me, and it scared me too. He just seemed out of control, unpredictable, and I was scared to be alone with him much longer.

So I kept getting dressed and getting my stuff together, and then he started really screaming at me. He hadn't touched me, and he wasn't being violent, but he was in my face screaming about how I can't leave him there with a fucking hard-on and he didn't pay three hundred dollars to have to finish off by hand. And how I was a shitty whore and he wasn't going to pay one cent and that I was lucky he wasn't charging me for all the coke

I did (even though I only did one line!). Then he called me a cokehead whore and said what could you expect from fucking crackhead whores (I was trying to figure out how I suddenly changed from being a cokehead to a crackhead), and how Miss Irma promised her whores were clean but clearly I was just a fucking addict and he was going to tell her to fire me. He was blocking my way to the door through most of this rant, and at some point I started crying a little.

This is the most ridiculous thing, but what started me crying is when he said I was a shitty whore who was no good at my job. Because I am good! I really do work hard at this. I've heard the jokes about how easy it is to make money on your back, but let me tell you, it is not easy. In addition to be dangerous and scary, it's actually a lot of work. And only a pretty small percentage of it is on my back. I always work hard and bring 100 percent to everything I do, and I just wish people appreciated the effort I put in.

He kept me there for quite some time, yelling at me for being a whore, for being a bad whore, for crying, for being a drug addict . . . anything he could think of. Called me fat and ugly too. And I just kept asking over and over, "Please let me through. Can I get through?" At one point I even started to take my clothes off again, in hopes that if I could just finish the date he would let me go, but that set him off again and he kept saying he didn't even want me and that I was no good and that he'd have more fun with a blow-up doll.

Anyway, finally he seemed to run out of steam and he wandered off to get a cigarette, so I made my escape. By then I was more than an hour late to get home, so I took a cab instead of wasting time on the bus. When I got home my mom asked where I'd been, and I didn't even bother to lie because I knew she would check any story I gave her about the bus breaking down or whatever. So I just didn't say anything and went up to my room and cried.

Today was awful, and now I'm terrified that Mom will use my outburst as an excuse to send me away. I better go downstairs with some story and make it up to her. But hey, at least I have a worst-date story now.

Thurs, Feb 19

Just when I thought things couldn't get any worse.

I went by Miss Irma's office today to pick up my fee, and Anne said she didn't have anything for me. I pointed out to her that I had an appointment clearly marked on the schedule and I needed to be paid for it, but she just said that if I thought there was some kind of mistake, I was free to take it up with Miss Irma. And she pointed me to Irma's door.

I didn't like the sound of that, but what choice did I have?

I went in to see her. Miss Irma started in right away about how furious the client was and how he had complained about me, so I tried to defend myself. I explained about how he had made me do drugs. Miss Irma asked if he had held me down and forced me, and I had to admit that he hadn't, but I did tell her about how he wouldn't let me go and how he was being abusive. Then she asked if he hit me, and I had to say no. She asked if he injured me in any way, but he hadn't.

So then she lectured me for a while about how important it is to keep the client happy at all times. And at the end she added, "Unless you are in danger," like it was an afterthought.

"I was!" I said. "He was threatening me and he wouldn't let me leave. And I was . . . I was scared."

Miss Irma was silent for a few moments, just looking at me over the top of her glasses.

"Of course," she said at last, "if you were in danger, you did the right thing. You must always leave if you don't feel safe."

I sighed with relief. "So you'll pay me?" I said.

Miss Irma smiled coldly. "How can I pay you if I did not get paid? Be reasonable."

"But you said—"

"The most important thing is to be safe. Surely your safety is more important to you than money."

"Yes," I said, "but—"

"You did the right thing. We all have to look after ourselves in this business."

"I thought . . . I thought we look out for each other."

Miss Irma laughed. "Who gave you that idea?" she said.

So on top of that being the worst date ever, I'm not even getting paid for it. And in fact, I'm in the hole since I blew money on the taxi home.

Fri, Feb 20

Chinese New Year. Normally this is my favorite time of the year, with so much good food, and firecrackers, and decorating the house. . . . But it's hard to celebrate family and community when I've spent the last few months making my parents hate me.

I'm really trying these days to stay in line and not give them a reason to make good on their threat, but it's hard. They just don't trust me anymore. Not that I can really blame them.

I know my parents would say that none of this would have happened if I could only have been the good, obedient girl they wanted, but sometimes I wonder if the problem is really that I've always been too obedient. Trying to live up to their expectations of the dutiful daughter nearly drove me crazy. I was living so much for other people, it hardly felt like living at all. Then I traded all that in for the "bad girl" life of a call girl, but even there, I spend all my time trying to be good, trying to be what people want, to fulfill their fantasies, to live up to Miss Irma's expectations, not to disappoint anyone. Where am I in all of this? What about me?

And what happens when all the people I am trying to obey disagree with each other? Or when obeying one person leads me in a bad direction? At a certain point, I have to start trusting myself and doing what I think is right, because the people around me don't always have my best interests at heart, or know what's best for me.

But then, how can I follow my own mind when I don't even know it? And how can I make the best decisions for myself when there's so much about the world I don't know?

I don't know, but after that last date, I am thinking again about quitting. Not for my parents, not for Ada, but because it might be the right thing for me. Maybe it's time to stop living in this crazy fantasy. Because it is starting to seem not so fantastic.

Wed, Feb 25

I haven't gotten called for another date since last payday. I'm guessing Miss Irma is mad at me for talking back and not just accepting whatever she says as law. But you know what? I'm just as glad. I'm still having nightmares about that last client, and when I even think about going out on another date, I just start to feel sick and panicky and my skin goes clammy. So I don't regret being left out of the loop for now.

The more I think about it, the more I realize I don't want to go back to that ever again. I had already been planning to quit at some point. I was just trying to save up enough money to have a nice amount for me and Ada. Since I didn't get paid for that last date, I have a little bit less than I'd been hoping for, but maybe it's enough. Maybe it has to be.

I'm going to call Ada and tell her about my plan. If she wants to talk me out of it, she can try, but I hope that she wants what I want. I just want to walk away from this mess and start over.

Wed, Feb 25, later

Just got off the phone with Ada. I'm still kind of . . . confused though.

I wanted to tell her my plan and hear her say, "Yes, we can do it. Let's make a new life for ourselves." Better yet, I wanted to hear that she had a better plan than mine, one that would solve all our problems. Or if she couldn't offer me any of that yet, I expected her to at least talk me out of quitting, so we could keep saving up. But nothing went quite how I expected.

"I'm glad you called," she said immediately upon answering the phone. "I need to talk to you."

"I need to talk to you too," I said, and before she could get in another word, I started in about my little dream of us living together in an apartment, getting real, legal jobs to support ourselves, and not getting pushed around by parents or Miss Irma or the clients anymore.

I kept talking for a while before I realized Ada hadn't said anything.

"Ada?" I said. "Are you there?" Still silence, but I could hear her breathing on the other end of the line. "Tell me what I should do, Ada. Should we quit? Or should we keep on with Miss Irma? I know we can trust her. I know she would never put us in any real harm, but—"

Ada barked out a humorless laugh.

"What?" I said. "What's going on?"

"Quit," she replied.

"What?"

"You should quit. You have to." Her voice sounded odd, broken. "I'm asking . . . I'm begging you."

"What's going on, Ada?"

"Nothing," she said with a sort of grim finality. "Nothing you need to worry about. I'm taking care of it, okay? It wasn't your fault, and it's not your problem. So don't worry about it."

"Okay, but Ada, did something happen? You sound upset." Actually, she sounded more than upset. She sounded scared.

"I'll be fine," she said. "I know what I'm doing. Just stay the hell away from Irma. Don't take any more dates. Don't respond if she contacts you. Ignore her, and she can't hurt you. In fact, take that stupid phone and throw it in the bay, like you wanted to that other time. I should have let you then. I should have made you do it then. Promise me you'll do it now."

"Okay. I promise. What's gotten into you? Why are you talking like this? Are you okay? Can I help?"

"I can't talk about it," she said, and hung up.

What was all that about? I'm worried about her.

Fri, Feb 27

I wish I knew what was going on with Ada. I've called and texted her a few times since the other day, but she's not answering. Not that that's all that unusual with her. Sometimes if she has a crisis with her mom or something, I won't hear from her for a couple of days. When I'm not working, we don't necessarily interact that much. And she's tough and smart. If anyone can take care of herself, it's Ada.

Still, something about my last conversation with her . . . I wish I knew what was going on. She sounded nervous and upset. A little desperate, even. But I trust her. And she did give me the answer I was looking for. I wanted her to tell me if I should quit the business or keep going a little longer, and she told me what I think I needed to hear. It's always tempting to work a little longer, turn just one more trick, in hopes of easy money, but the money's not so easy, and as I learned from my last date, sometimes there's no money at all.

I'm glad she said what she did. Quitting's hard, but I think it was the right decision. That lifestyle is not healthy. It grinds you down. I didn't even do it very long, and it has already taken its toll on me. And if I'm not doing it, at least it's easier for me to be obedient to my parents, so I don't have to worry about them sending me to Taiwan.

I just wish I knew what Ada thought about the other part of the plan . . . about us moving in together. All the time I was dreaming it, I don't think I ever allowed myself to wonder what I would do if Ada said no. If she wasn't interested. But what if she's sick of me? What if she'd rather live with someone like Jen? Someone cooler and more sophisticated? What if she just wants me to quit because she has figured out I'm not cut out for that kind of life, and she wants to just hang out with people more like her?

I don't know. Maybe she's right. Maybe to Ada it's really obvious how stupid my plan is and how I'm just too sheltered and ignorant to survive on my own. Maybe she knows I could never make it work and was trying to let me down easy.

Mon, March 2

I am trying very hard to be good, but it really sucks being on lockdown. My parents are sticking to their plan of not letting me go anywhere or do anything except for schoolwork. I'm so far behind in everything. I've missed so much. As overwhelmed as I used to feel by school, it's ten times worse now.

And it's not just the work. Back at the beginning of the year, I thought I knew what it meant to be invisible. I felt like a loser, an outcast, like no one really noticed me. I didn't know how good I had it back then. I had my regular table at lunch and I was in all those activities—no matter how I felt, I was part of the fabric of the school.

That's all gone now. I'm embarrassed to talk to my old friends, and they don't really seem to miss me. And Ada hasn't been coming to school, so other than answering the occasional question in class, I basically don't talk to or interact with anyone all day long. I'm like a ghost, haunting the halls of the high school.

There is something comforting in the ritual of it, though. I mean, as bad as it is, at least I don't have to worry about people assaulting me or making me do drugs I don't want. It's boring and frustrating, but it's not so scary. Scary was exciting at first, but I think I had enough. I'm still having nightmares about that last client.

I'm starting to get worried about Ada, too. I haven't heard from her in almost a week. I know she told me to throw Miss Irma's phone in the ocean, and I was going to sneak out of school and do it the other day, but I decided not to. What if Ada tries to contact me on it? She has my other number, but if she's in trouble, she might not have a chance to try both numbers, and if there is any chance she might try to reach me through Irma's phone, well, I'd never forgive myself if I wasn't there for her when she needed me.

It does make me nervous when I see it in my purse, but so far Irma hasn't contacted me on it since our last meeting, and that suits me just fine.

Mon, March 2, later

I convinced my parents to let me start swimming again! Not with the team. I don't know if I even want that anymore, but I really miss having something to do that was just for me. One thing in my life where I don't have to do what people tell me or care what they want. When I'm swimming, it's just me and the water.

I told them that my body was going to atrophy if they kept me locked up all the time, so they finally decided that I could go to the YMCA pool in the evenings. Only an hour, though, so it won't interfere with my homework. And they'll drop me off and pick me up. That's what they say, anyway. I know they're really afraid of me sneaking off.

I'm so excited to get back in the water again!

Fri, March 6

I feel gross.

I don't know what to do. I need to talk to someone, but who? I wish I could talk to Ada, but I still can't get in touch with her.

I thought things were supposed to be okay now. I thought if I just stuck to my parents' plan and behaved myself and did everything they told me to, I'd be safe and I'd never have to deal with the scary situations that hooking put me in. But it's like I can't go back to who I was. I should explain what happened. Maybe that will help me calm down.

I've been going to the pool every day all week now. It was nice. It didn't make everything better, but for an hour a day, at least I knew no one would be telling me what to do or hassling me or expecting stuff from me. That's what I thought, anyway.

So today I was doing some laps, not even trying for speed or perfect form or anything, just enjoying the feel of the water on my skin. And it was just a bit before closing, so I had the whole pool to myself. I was vaguely aware that there was someone standing nearby, but I didn't really pay attention, because I was off in my own little blue world. Soon I noticed the person had gotten in the water and was swimming next to me. He was really good, matching me easily, stroke for stroke, which is unusual given that most people at this pool are old folks or little kids.

So I stopped when I finished my lap and I looked up, and guess who it was.

Tyler Adams.

I wasn't expecting that at all. I felt like someone had just knocked the wind out of me. And even weirder than running into him at the pool was that he was actually looking at me and smiling, as if he knew who I was. Which was weird but sort of . . . nice, after everything that happened. These past couple of weeks I've been so isolated and alone, not speaking to anyone except my parents and everyone at school looking through me like I'm invisible. It felt nice to have someone treat me like I'm human.

And I couldn't help remembering how I used to feel about him. It's not like I could just instantly go back to that little-girl crush, not after everything I've been through, but there's no denying how good Tyler looks. A lot better-looking than the men I'm used to being with these days.

So we got to talking. I worried it would be superawkward and I would act like an idiot, just like I used to, but I guess at least one positive side effect of my recent career is I am less tongue-tied around boys. We talked about the swim team a bit and how they were doing, and I gave him a lame excuse for why I wasn't swimming with them anymore. Eventually I was like, "I better hit the shower. My ride will be here soon." And he put a hand on my arm and said, "Don't. Not yet." And he gave me this smile. I've seen him give that smile to other girls, but I never dreamed he would use it on me.

I admit, I melted a little. I stayed in the pool, and when he ducked into my lane and pressed up close to me, I didn't stop him. It was late, but the water was warm and the lights were glowing and it was almost romantic. And then he pulled in closer and started kissing me.

I was surprised, but too turned-on to really think too much about it. All that was going through my head was, *I wonder if it can really be this easy.* Tyler wasn't a client, and he wasn't twice my age or more, and he wasn't paunchy or bald. He's just a cute boy my age who likes me and wants to kiss me. And maybe I deserve that, after all I've been through. Maybe that would be the perfect antidote to all the gross stuff I've had to do for the past few months. Maybe I can just be with Tyler and be normal and happy, and it can all be uncomplicated.

That was what I was thinking until he stopped kissing me and started whispering in my ear. At first it was nice things, or nice enough. He was telling me how sexy I was and how much he wanted to touch me. He was moving pretty fast, I know, but the truth is, I wanted to touch him too.

But then he started saying other things like, "I bet you know all kinds of tricks. I bet you could make it good." I didn't know what he was talking about, but I started to feel uncomfortable. He was pressed all up against me now, and he said, "Why don't you show me what you know?"

So I was like, "What do you mean?"

"Don't play coy," he said. "I know what you are. I saw you hanging around with Ada Culver. You're like her, aren't you? You used to be a little nerd, but she made you a whore just like her."

I didn't like that. I didn't like him talking about Ada that way, so I stopped kissing and touching him and tried to wriggle away, but he had me pressed pretty firmly against the wall of the pool with his arms around me like a cage.

"Come on," he said in a whisper. "Don't try to act like you're some virgin." His lips were moving against my ear, and I could feel him pressed up between my legs. And he started whispering to me about Ada, how he had found out about her. He told me his uncle was one of her clients, and he had told Tyler all about her one day when he was drunk.

"My uncle's a real sleazebag," he said. "He told me all the things he did with Ada, all the things he made her do to him.

Why don't you show me what she taught you? I can pay, if you want. Then you'll be my little whore to do whatever I want with."

For a while I was just frozen, listening to him whisper those horrible words in my ear. I didn't know what to think. I felt like such an idiot, like I had been so naive. For so long I'd let myself believe I was living in two different worlds . . . that I had these two identities, but they were totally separate. On one hand, I was a highly paid call girl. On the other, I was an ordinary high school student, unpopular but high achieving. But that was a mistake, or a lie, because it was only one life all along. The same stinking life.

If Tyler knows about me, how many other people know? How many has he told? How many will he tell? What happens when Jenny and Eiko and John find out? What about the teachers? And my parents?

Finally I came back to myself and shoved Tyler away from me. He let me go without a fight, but his smug laughter echoed through the empty hall as I dragged myself out of the water.

Since then I have showered and toweled off and returned home and crawled into bed, but somehow I still can't stop shivering. What do I do now? Throughout this whole thing, I've always believed that there was a safety net. If I wanted to, I could pretend this was all a bad dream and just go back to the ordinary life I had before. But that's not possible anymore. Tyler had called me a dirty little whore. What's the point in getting offended? It was true. These aren't just words. This is who I am.

Sat, March 7

My phone is ringing. The pink phone.

It's like everything I have tried to do to walk away from that existence is falling apart around me. First that horrible experience with Tyler, so I don't even feel safe in the water anymore. I told my parents I don't want to go back to the pool again, and of course they are confused since I bargained so hard for this. Why don't I want it all of a sudden? And what can I say to them? But what does it matter even? They are going to find out all about me soon anyway. Now that Tyler knows, it's only a matter of time.

And now Irma's phone is ringing. And it's not Ada.

I don't understand it because usually when they want to set up a date, I get a text from Anne, or sometimes from Irma. And only if I ignore that, then they'll call. But there was no text this time, just a ringing phone. Even though I haven't heard from Ada in more than a week, I remember her last words to me. I remember how she told me not to talk to Irma ever again, to quit, to ignore all her attempts to contact me, to throw the phone into the bay.

So I won't answer. They called back three times in twenty minutes, but now it's been two hours with no calls, so maybe I am off the hook.

Sat, March 7, later

Phone is ringing again. I'm just staring at it, not answering. I mean, for all they know, I could have thrown it into the bay. I don't have to answer it.

It's weird, though. . . . Somehow, every time it rings, I feel like Miss Irma can see me.

Mon, March 9

They found me. I guess it didn't matter that I didn't answer the phone, because they just found another way to get to me. Now I'm in a mess, but maybe I can help Ada at least.

The phone kept ringing yesterday, and this morning while I was in school. It was getting more and more frequent, but I kept ignoring it.

Then, after school today, I was walking toward the buses and I happened to glance over to where Miss Irma's cars used to pick up me and Ada to take us to our dates. And there it was: Irma's car. At the sight of it, I sort of froze and stared. I certainly didn't have a date scheduled, and Ada hadn't been on the school grounds in almost two weeks, so who was it there for? I wondered if someone else at the school had started hooking. Maybe one of the younger kids. But some part of me knew that was not what was going on. I just had this dark sense, like something bad was about to happen, and all I could think to do was get away. I put my head down and forced myself to keep walking toward the buses, but I didn't make it more than a few steps before I heard someone call my name. More on instinct than by choice, I stopped and turned.

It was a big, solidly built man. Definitely not someone usually on the school grounds, but he looked strangely familiar. He said my name again, and that's when it clicked into place—I'd seen him at the Valentine's party. He was one of Miss Irma's security force. The people Ada had referred to as "goons." The people Ada had warned me about.

"You better come with me," said the man.

My feet felt frozen to the pavement. Everything in my body was screaming at me to get away from this situation. As long as I was here at the school, this crowd of students swarming around me, there wasn't much this man could do to me. Following him into that car, I'd be putting myself at risk. Of what, I wasn't sure. I couldn't think of anything Miss Irma would want to do to me, or why, but I couldn't ignore Ada's warning. Something had scared her, and that was enough to scare me.

Again he asked me to come with him. Calmly, quietly, but with just a hint of a threat.

I wanted to tell him no, but I couldn't find the words, so I just shook my head and turned away, back toward the buses. Then I heard his voice again.

"It's about Ada."

I turned around. "Is she all right?"

"I think you'd better come with me."

So I went. What choice did I have? Yes, it was risky and scary and I had no clue what I was getting myself into, but if there was any chance of finding out what happened to Ada, of helping her if she was in trouble, there was no way I was going to refuse that.

Once at the downtown office, Anne met me and showed me in to Miss Irma.

"I'm so glad you came," she said. "I got worried when you ignored my messages."

"I'm sorry about that," I said. "I can return the phone. I've . . . I've decided to get out of the business."

Irma looked slightly surprised. "Of course," she said. "You are free to leave anytime you want, as I said. But maybe you should keep the phone for now." That sounded a bit ominous. "It is inconvenient when people lose track of their phones," Irma went on. "You know I worry about my employees. I like to check on them, make sure they are okay. I'm very worried about Ada, because she doesn't answer her phone this past week. But perhaps you can tell me where she is."

My heart sank. I had hoped Irma would tell me where Ada was.

"I don't know anything about Ada," I said. "I haven't heard from her in a while."

"I see," said Irma. "Are you sure, though? Think hard."

What could I say or do to convince Miss Irma I had even less information than she did? When I didn't answer right away, Miss Irma changed her tack.

"Don't play dumb. You're in this together."

That had me confused.

"In what?" I said.

"I am not unreasonable," Irma went on. "I'm not some violent gangster. I'm a businesswoman. I respect free enterprise. I admire Ada's ambition to go into business for herself. We all have to start somewhere. But one thing I do not accept is poaching clients. Damon is my client, not yours. You girls think you are the attraction, but you are easily replaced. I earned my cut of your little scheme, and I want it."

So that's what this was about: Damon. I should have guessed. But how did she find out? Of course, my big mouth at the Valentine's party. She could have heard me, or anyone there could have blabbed to her. So this really was all my fault, then.

"We didn't earn anything," I rushed to explain to Irma. "It wasn't like that. I swear. It was a freebie. Ada was just setting a couple of friends up on a date. We didn't charge him."

I only realized once the words left my mouth how unlikely my story sounded, even though it was true. The look on Miss Irma's face showed that she was thinking the same thing.

"Really?" she said with more than a hint of sarcasm. "A whore and her virgin friend seduce a rich young client and no money changed hands?" Miss Irma shook her head. "Maybe an innocent idiot like you could wander into this situation by accident, but Ada is not so stupid. She knows very well the price of a virgin. She's far too clever to let that slide, even for a friend."

"I promise you it's true," I said a little desperately. "There was no money."

"Save your pleas," she said with an airy wave of the hand. "It doesn't matter one way or the other. It's not my fault if you were too stupid to charge him. I'm still owed the money I should have gotten. Ada owes me a debt and she ran out on it, so now you owe me a debt. Either pay me, or find Ada for me so she can pay me. Your choice."

So that was it. That was why Ada wasn't returning my calls. But that meant that if I could solve this problem, if I could settle her debt, she could come back.

I asked Miss Irma how much it was. When I heard the amount, I had a moment of relief combined with hopelessness. I have it . . . or almost. It's just a little bit more than I have saved for the apartment I was going to get with Ada. But handing it over to Miss Irma means the death of that fantasy, once and for all.

Well, since Ada's not speaking to me, I guess it was pretty much dead anyway.

I told Miss Irma I could get her the money. She looked surprised, and more than a little suspicious.

"You can? When?"

"I can pay you now," I said. "Or tomorrow," I corrected myself. "I just need to run home and get it."

Irma looked at me closely.

"You've been saving your pennies," she observed. I didn't say anything. "I underestimated you," she went on. "You're not as stupid as I thought, though you should pick your friends more carefully in the future. You can save all the money in the world, but it won't be any good if your friends skip town and leave you with their debts."

My face burned at the insult, but I tried to stay focused. "Ada skipped town?" This was the information I had come for

Miss Irma shrugged delicately. "As far as I know. My people have searched the whole city for her. If you think you know where she might be, by all means, hunt her down. As long as I get my money, it's all the same to me."

I have an appointment to drop off the necessary cash at Miss Irma's office in just under twenty-four hours. I've pulled my little savings from under my bed and counted it all out on the covers. I'm almost there but not quite. I hate to do this, but I think I'm going to have to sneak some bills out of my mom's mah-jongg jar. I know it's wrong, but I don't even know what Miss Irma's goons might do to me or Ada if I don't pay up. And I don't really want to find out.

Can I really do this? I have the money, but it's every last bit I saved. All my dreams for the future and all my hopes of escaping this awful life. What do I do after this? Go back to Miss Irma and start taking dates again, try to build it back up? But what's the point, with Ada gone? Without the money and without her, I don't even know what my dream is anymore.

Can it really be that what Miss Irma said is true? That Ada abandoned me to deal with this debt on my own, so she wouldn't have to? Of course, she did warn me not to talk to Miss Irma ever again. I guess she was hoping I could just avoid the problem and slip quietly back into my old life. But she must have known Miss Irma's goons would come after me. Why didn't she just come to me? If she had told me the situation, we could have fixed it together.

I called and texted her to let her know that I am paying her debt and that she's in the clear, but I just keep getting voice mail. I don't understand why she doesn't respond.

This is driving me crazy. I have to know what happened to her. I'm sure Miss Irma's goons have already checked Ada's house, but maybe her mom will be able to tell me something. It can't hurt to ask.

Mon, March 9, later

I'm at Ada's house. It was stupid to come here. I don't know what I expected to learn. Obviously Ada wasn't going to just be sitting here, watching TV. And if I was hoping her mom would be able to give me some clues, it doesn't look like that's going to happen.

When I got here, it was almost eerie how normal the place looked. Just sitting there in the gathering shadows of dusk, like all the other houses on the streets. The lights were on, giving it a cozy glow, and the twilight hid the shabbiness and disrepair of the place. I knocked on the door and waited a bit but didn't hear anything. I started to wonder if Ada's mom could have gone out and left all the lights on. I was about to give up and walk away when I heard a sound from inside the house. I held my breath and listened. Someone was definitely inside. Heart hammering, I raised my hand to knock once more, but just then I heard another sound, this time much closer. A door latch.

The door opened, but only a crack. The chain was still done up, preventing the door from opening more than a couple of inches. Behind it stood a haggard, anxious-eyed woman who I assumed to be Ada's mother.

"Hi!" I said brightly, trying to seem as nonthreatening as possible. "I'm a friend of Ada's. I used to come by and visit sometimes, but I don't think we ever met."

Ada's mom didn't say anything, but her eyes slid up and down my body, drawing in every detail. I couldn't tell if I was winning her over.

"I was just wondering if . . ." I hesitated. How much did Ada's mom know? How much should I give away, and how much should I hold back? I decided to keep it simple for now. "Do you know where she is?"

"Do you know where she is?" she said in a cracked, wavering voice.

I shifted uncomfortably. I honestly couldn't tell if she was asking me about Ada's whereabouts or just repeating what I said, as if she barely spoke the language but was trying out the sounds.

"No," I answered at last, trying to keep my voice calm and neutral. "I don't know, but I am looking for her. Do you remember when you last saw her? Do you know how to get in touch with her?"

"You're not one of them, are you?" she said. "You don't seem like one of them. Unless you're trying to trick me."

"One of who?" I wondered if she'd had some run-in with Miss Irma's goons. That might explain some of her behavior. "Have people been here, looking for Ada? Other people?"

"I think they got her," she said, leaning forward to whisper conspiratorially. "They were looking for her and then they must have come and taken her away."

"Taken her away?" I said. "Who took her away? When? What did they look like?"

I didn't want to stress her out or put too much pressure on her clearly fragile psyche, but I had to know what she had seen. I was feeling frantic. Was she talking about Miss Irma's goons? But if they had come and taken Ada away, why would they ask me where she is? Who else would be looking for Ada? Who would take her away? The police? Or was it possible that she was mixed up in something else?

"Please," I said. "Try to remember. Who took her away? If you remember anything at all . . ."

The woman shook her head. "You should stay away, if you know what's good for you. It's dangerous here."

"Dangerous?"

"We're being watched," she whispered hoarsely. "You have to act normal because they are always watching."

"Who is watching? The people who took Ada?" Instinctively, I jerked my head around to look up and down the street, but everything looked normal.

"She might be working for them. I didn't want to believe it either, not at first, but I don't think I can trust her."

She had figured out Ada was working for Miss Irma, then. That made some sense, even if she was confused about the details.

"Did she tell you where she was going?"

"She went with them, or they took her, or she is spying on me for them. I don't think I can trust her. She was always watching me, but I don't think it's her fault. They got to her."

"Who got to her?" I asked, growing desperate for any real information.

"Tom," said the woman in an anxious whisper.

"Tom?" I repeated. "Tom who?"

"He got to her, just like he got to Katie. Tom and Angelina and Miley. They're planning something. It's got something to do with me, but I don't know what yet. I tried to get Ada to help, but she was working for them already, watching me and reporting to them. I used to follow their messages to each other on the Internet, but then I realized they could see me too, so I had to stop. I turned it off, but that made them angry. That's when they got to Ada."

185

With a sick feeling in my stomach, I suddenly remembered all the celebrity gossip magazines I had noticed when I had visited Ada in the past. It was impossible to tell how much of my conversation with Ada's mom had been based in fact and how much based in her paranoid delusions. Ada had told me that her mom had "episodes," and she had hinted that they were getting worse. It seemed as though she was in the middle of a bad one.

I wondered if that was part of why Ada had left. Maybe even more than her debt to Miss Irma. If her mom had turned on her, had decided that Ada was part of some master conspiracy against her, that could be pretty hard to live with.

In any case, it was becoming pretty clear that I wasn't going to get any solid information out of Ada's mom, and the longer I talked to her, the more I risked her slotting me in with whoever else might be out to "get" her. I thanked her for her time and let her close the door. Now I'm sitting on the garden wall under a streetlamp, trying to decide what to do next. I guess this is a dead end, like I thought it would be. I'll try texting Ada one more time, letting her know I'm here. If she ever does check her messages, she'll at least know I cared enough to look.

That's weird. Something just caught my eye. Now I'm not even sure if I really saw anything, or if Ada's mom's delusions have gone to my head, but I could have sworn I saw a flash of

186

light from that window. The window to Ada's bedroom. It's the only room in the house with no light on, but it looks like something flickered in there. Would it be crazy if I crept over there and peeked in the window?

Mon, March 9, later

Wow. That was the craziest thing I've ever done. Well, other than getting paid to have sex with strangers. Maybe my life is so weird now, I've lost all sense of proportion.

I went over to Ada's window after I saw that flash and I peered in, but it was all dark in there and I could barely make anything out. I don't even know exactly what I was expecting to see, but it definitely didn't look like Ada was in there. I was about to give up and go back home, but I couldn't stop turning the question over in my mind. What had I seen flash in there? Was it just my imagination? What would give off that kind of blue light?

Then I noticed the light again, but this time it wasn't coming from Ada's room. It was coming from my purse. It was my phone lighting up as a text came through. My parents, wanting to know where the hell I was. My first thought was panic that they had noticed I was gone too long, but before I could think too much about that, I realized something else. The flash of light I had seen had to be Ada's phone!

I tried Ada's phone again, calling this time. Sure enough,

a blueish light came on, illuminating Ada's room dimly as I listened to the ringtone. So Ada had abandoned her phone at home, which meant all my messages had gone unread. I felt my heart sink a little at this realization, but then another thought occurred to me. If I had Ada's phone, it might give me another clue as to where she was hiding.

Not really dreaming it would work, I gave the window a little shove and it moved. Ada must have left it unlocked. I checked around, looking up and down the street, my heart beating wildly at what I was about to do. But everything seemed quiet. As silently as possible, I slid the window up and hoisted myself up and inside. I gave a quick look around for any other possible clues, but I didn't want to stick around too long and risk getting caught by Ada's mom, so I just grabbed the phone and got out of there.

Now I'm on a bus headed back home and not totally sure what to do with my trophy. I thought it might be useful to see who Ada had spoken to last, but the last calls in her logs were me and Miss Irma. No new information there. Should I just start calling random people from her address book? I don't know if that might make things better or worse.

Jen's number is in here. At least I kind of know her. I'm not sure what she could possibly know that would be a help at this point, but it's worth a shot.

Mon, March 9, later

I texted Jen twice and called once, but she's not responding. Why doesn't anyone pick up their phones? What do I do? Do I give up?

I'm almost home now, but the minute I walk in the door, my parents are going to start talking about sending me away. How can I let them do that when Ada is so clearly in trouble? I've got to do something.

Should I try another number? Or Jen's address is in here. I suppose I could go over there. Maybe she'll be more willing to talk to me face-to-face.

Mon, March 9, later

That didn't go exactly as planned, but at least I have a new direction now.

I made my way over to South Downtown and found my way to Jen's place through a maze of old abandoned warehouses. When I found the building, it had a roll-up door, and I wondered if the owners even knew it was being used as living space. I banged on the door for a while until finally Jen's roommate, Beth, came down. I asked if Jen was there, but Beth just said, "Nope."

"Do you know when she'll be back?"

"Nope."

I was getting frustrated.

"Can I come in and wait for her, then? I really need to talk to her."

"You could be waiting a while," said Beth, lounging calmly in the doorway. "Jen's in jail. She got picked up last night."

I have to admit, that was the last thing I was expecting.

"For what?" I asked.

Beth laughed. "What do you think? Or were you unaware that your chosen profession is illegal? This could happen to any of us."

"Sure," I said, "but we're not streetwalkers. And Irma . . ."

"Irma only protects people as long as they're useful to her," Beth said, her voice hard. "Irma kicked Jen off the payroll two weeks ago because of her drug problem, so she started posting ads for her services online. One of the clients she got was a setup. They had sex, she asks for her money, and the guy whips out a badge instead."

"A cop would really do that?"

"You watch too much TV," she said. "Not all cops are heroes."

"Will she go to prison?"

"At sixteen?" said Beth. "Not likely. Probably she'll have to go to juvie, or she'll get stuck in the social services system or something. Either way, it will be a pain in the ass. What really sucks is how am I going to make rent without a roommate?"

At this point, I was almost on the point of crying from

frustration and worry. I leaned against the doorframe with all the fight gone out of me.

Beth narrowed her eyes. "What do you want with Jen, anyway? You guys aren't friends."

"I don't want Jen. I want Ada. I mean, I'm looking for her. She disappeared."

"She's not answering her phone?"

"No." I held up Ada's phone. "Look, do you know anything? I know you're not her biggest fan, but this is important."

Beth huffed a breath. "I bet it is. Everyone's always worried about Ada. I wouldn't be that worried about her. She knows how to take care of herself."

"What do you mean? If you know something, you have to tell me."

"You shouldn't trust her, you know. She'll take advantage of you just like she does everyone else."

I shook my head. "She wouldn't do that."

"Wouldn't she? You'll realize someday that I did you a favor. Ada was manipulating you and trying to put one over on Irma. She's done it before."

"A favor?" I repeated. "What kind of . . . ?" Suddenly I understood. "It was you," I said slowly. "You heard me talking at the Valentine's party about what happened between me and Damon. You went to Miss Irma."

"I wasn't trying to cause trouble for you," said Beth, looking sullen. "I was trying to protect you. Ada's a bad egg. You're better off without her."

"You're wrong. Ada would never do anything . . ."

"She got you into this life, didn't she? You're not like us. Me and Jen and Ada and the others . . . We didn't have much of a choice. Miss Irma looks like a walk in the park compared to the other options life gave us. But you could have been something. You had a good life and opportunities. Money, a future, a family that loves you. Ada couldn't stand it. She wanted to bring you down to our level."

Almost against my will, I thought about her words. Was it true what she was saying? Was it Ada's fault I got into this life? But I'd wanted to. I'd practically begged her, and she had always tried to stop me.

"Listen," I said, "I don't care what she did. If you know anything at all, you have to help me. Ada could be in serious trouble, and we need to look out for each other. Did she come by here? Did Jen mention that she'd spoken to her recently?"

Beth shook her head.

"Great," I said. "Dead end. Thanks anyway."

I turned my coat collar up and stepped back into the driving rain, tears of frustration prickling behind my eyes.

"Wait," said Beth. I turned around. "Before you give up, you might as well try Westlake Park."

"What have you heard?" I said sharply.

"I swear, I don't know anything. She could be a million miles away now, or around the corner, or dead, but Westlake Park is where a lot of Irma's old whores wash up when Irma's through with them. You could call it the Miss Irma Retirement Community."

I don't know what that means, but I'm off to find out.

Mon, March 9, later

Westlake Park is right in the middle of downtown Seattle, blocks away from the art museum and the convention center. Minutes from the business hotels where I used to meet most of my clients and only a few steps away from where I walked with Damon on our date. I've passed this park dozens of time and never noticed anything strange about it. I was always here in daylight, and it seemed perfectly nice.

But it's different after dark, and it didn't take me long to figure out why Beth thought Ada might be here. The women standing around the park are obviously streetwalkers. That's what she meant by Miss Irma's Retirement Community. When girls like me and Ada and Beth get too old or too difficult for Miss Irma's service, this is the only option left.

Still, even if I understood what Beth had meant, it's hard to picture Ada in this environment. These girls don't dress like Ada. They're streetwalkers, and they are dressed to make sure everyone knows it. They lean into car windows, negotiating deals.

I walked around the park a few times, my eyes instinctively seeking out Ada's tall, graceful form, her long swirling coat, her shimmery blond hair. But is that what she would look like now? Or would she be dressed in hot pants and fishnets and a lace bra? Would she wear a wig, as many of the girls seem to? I watched everyone carefully, trying to see past their performance to the person underneath.

Unfortunately, it wasn't long before people started to notice me. A couple of the girls started staring back. One wanted to know what I was looking at and what my problem was. I wanted to run away, but I knew that wouldn't get me any closer to Ada. So I screwed up my courage and approached her.

"I'm looking for someone named Ada," I said. "Maybe you can help?" I pulled up a photo of her on my phone, but the woman wouldn't even look at it.

"I mind my own business around here, and so should you," she said.

I swallowed my disappointment and slinked away, wondering if anyone else would be more helpful. That's when someone grabbed me roughly by the arm and spun me around.

"What's a pretty girl like you doing in the park tonight?" This time it was a guy in his twenties with a hood up, shading his eyes. "Are you working tonight?"

I tried to tell him no, that I was just there looking for a friend, but he sneered.

"I've heard that before. Who are you working for?"

"No one," I stuttered. "I mean, I used to work for Miss Irma, but I'm just . . ."

"This park isn't up for grabs, you know. No free agents. Now, if you're unattached, I'd be happy to . . ."

"Thank you," I said, hurrying away from him. "I was just leaving."

I wandered into a darker, more deserted area, far from the corners where the cars pulled up, and now I'm just sitting here, trying to stay out of everyone's way and figure out my next move. If I keep hanging around and asking questions, obviously I'm going to get myself into trouble, but I can't give up on Ada yet! Is there anywhere else I could look for her? Anyone else who might be willing to help?

Crap. There's a guy who has been lurking in the shadows near me for the last few minutes, and he is making me seriously nervous. Maybe I should find a different place to sit.

Tues, March 10? I think?

I am so confused. I wish I could remember exactly what happened last night and how I ended up here, but I'm only getting weird flashes, and I'm not sure what's real and what's a dream.

I'm in a bed right now, and from the light outside the window, I think it's very early morning. But it's not my bed, and it's not a hospital bed. Where am I?

I'd better try to reconstruct what happened after my last entry.

The guy lurking in my previous entry . . . I remember him. Just as I was thinking of moving, he walked up and asked if I had any money. I said, "Sorry, no," and he said, "Are you sure?"

I ignored him and started to walk away, but then he said, "How about you let me check?" I should have kept moving, but I chanced a glance at him and that's when I saw he had a knife. I kind of froze at that point. All I could think about was the envelope full of cash in my purse. The money I had saved up for ages. The money that was supposed to be the nest egg for my life with Ada. The money I had promised to deliver to Miss Irma tomorrow, to make sure Ada would be safe.

I started to walk away again, out of the shadows and toward a better-lit area, but the man grabbed my clothes and tugged me back toward him until I could feel the end of his blade against my back. I tried to struggle and cry out, but . . .

I don't know what happened then. Everything gets hazy at that point.

The next thing I remember is a familiar voice talking, saying my name, and hands shaking me awake. I opened my eyes to see who it was. It wasn't Ada. It was Shawn. The beautiful boy from Miss Irma's Valentine's party.

But that can't be right, can it? I must have been dreaming. But whose bed am I in right now?

Tues, March 10? later

I just investigated a bit, trying to figure out what the hell is going on. I'm still wearing all my clothes from last night, but my purse is gone. Which means all the money is gone. Not just that, but my cell phone, and Ada's too. At least I still have this journal—I was writing in my journal when I saw the guy, so I still had it in my hands when I went down.

I don't know what to do. I still don't know where I am. The room I'm in is a strange combination of shabby and swank. There are water stains and cracks in the plaster and the blinds are broken and hanging off the window, but there is also a huge flat-screen TV at the foot of the bed and these sheets are nicer than the ones on my bed at home.

The view out the window is totally unfamiliar. It doesn't look anything like the area around Westlake Park. Should I try to sneak out of this place and find my way back home? But what then? Irma's goons will be looking for me by nightfall, and now I have nothing to offer them. Leading them to my house will only put my parents in danger. They don't deserve that.

And even if I get out of that mess, it's guaranteed now that my parents will send me to Taiwan the first chance they get.

I wish I could go back to the days when everything felt like a choice. When I got to decide every day whether I was going to pick the dangerous path or the safe one. That safe path doesn't seem to exist anymore, and the dangerous one is more dangerous than ever.

I hear noises outside the door. Whoever's apartment this is seems to have gotten up. I wish I knew whether I'm his prisoner or not.

Tues, March 10, later

So this really is Shawn's apartment, and that really was Shawn from the Valentine's party moving around in the front room. He just came in and brought me a breakfast sandwich. I ate a few bites but had to stop when I suddenly felt really queasy. Shawn said it was probably from bumping my head pretty hard last night. That explains the painful lump and the memory loss, at least.

He asked me a lot of questions about how I was feeling and if I remembered my name and stuff. I kept trying to interrupt him to ask him what the hell he was doing in that park and what exactly happened, but he shushed me and told me not to worry about it for now. He said I needed rest and he didn't want to wear me out, but that we would talk more later.

I really feel like I would rest better if I weren't so confused. But I am awfully sleepy.

Tues, March 10, later

Shawn just came in and brought me half a burrito. I assured him I was feeling much better, so he finally agreed to tell me a bit about last night.

He said he was just hanging out in the park when he heard shouting and saw someone get knocked down. He ran over and found me there. He says he couldn't have been more shocked when he saw it was me. Small world, I guess. I would never have expected to run into him in a place like that either, but I guess that's what Beth was trying to tell me. Everyone who works with Irma winds up there sooner or later.

I asked him if he knew who beat me up, but he said the guy was making a run for it by the time he got there, and he thought it was more important to help me than follow him.

"Do you think anyone else who was there might know who he was?" I asked. "Or where I could find him?"

Shawn frowned. "I doubt it. I don't know if you noticed, but people who hang out at that park tend to keep their eyes to themselves. You know what I mean?"

Of course I did. I remember how people acted last night when I asked about Ada. I started to nod in answer, but instead I burst into tears. Shawn sat down on the bed with me.

"What's the matter?" he said. "You're safe now."

So I explained to him about the money and the phones.

"You had an envelope full of cash? In Westlake Park after dark? I'm sorry, kid," he said, "but that wasn't a very intelligent plan. What were you even doing there?"

"Miss Irma says we owe her money," I explained. "A lot of money. Ada disappeared, I'm not sure why, but maybe because she couldn't pay what Irma was asking. But I have the money. I was trying to find her to tell her I have it and we can go pay Irma and it will all be okay. Except I was saving that money for an apartment, and now I'm back to zero, and now someone stole the money so actually I'm still in debt and Miss Irma's goons are going to start looking for me and I still don't know where Ada is or if she's okay and everything is wrong and I wish I were dead."

"Hey," said Shawn soothingly, "don't worry, all right? Just rest for now. You lost some money. You owe some money. It happens. It's not the end of the world. I promise. You're okay now, so just relax."

"But what about Ada?"

"Let me worry about Ada. I have better resources than you do to figure out what happened to her. I'll put the word out, and it will only be a matter of time before we hear something. Trust me. I know how to get information."

Which made something occur to me. "What were you doing in the park last night?"

Shawn smiled. "I'm there pretty much every night. Keeping an eye on some friends, you could say. You're not the only girl who likes to get into trouble around here, you know."

"So, what . . . ? You're some kind of guardian angel or something?"

Shawn laughed. "Never been called that before. But that's one way to look at it."

Fri, March 13

I'm still at Shawn's. He just came in with half of a submarine sandwich he saved for me. He's sweet, but I get the feeling that all he eats is fast food.

I told him I'm feeling a lot better now. I have to start thinking about what comes next. What am I going to do about Miss Irma? And how am I going to find Ada?

"Relax," said Shawn. "I told you to let me take care of it, and I did."

"What do you mean?"

"You don't have to worry about Miss Irma anymore. I got her off your back. Her goons won't be sniffing around anymore."

201

"What? But why not? What did you do?"

"I paid her," he said simply.

"You paid her?" I said, incredulous. "You paid her what we owed? But it was a lot of money!"

"That's all relative. A lot of money to you is just a sound investment to me."

I took a second to process that. At first I felt like a huge weight had just been lifted from me. I hadn't even realized how worried I was about Miss Irma and the debt. But after a moment that good feeling got swept away by a low, sinking one.

"That's really kind of you," I said. "Too kind. How will I ever pay you back?"

"Don't worry about it," said Shawn. "Think of it like karma. Or like you said back at Miss Irma's party."

"What did I say?"

"We need to look out for each other."

I managed a smile at this, but the phrase only reminded me of my other problem.

"What about Ada, then?" I said. "Any news?"

Shawn shifted and dropped his eyes. "Not yet," he said.

I didn't like the look on his face when he said that. I had a feeling he knew more than he was letting on, and I was desperate to hear whatever it was. But when I pressed him for more information, he just told me to get some more rest and left me alone in his bedroom.

Sat, March 14

I got it out of him. Now I know what it was Shawn was trying to hide from me.

Ada . . . I can't say it. I can't write it. It's stupid, but it feels like that would make it real. Maybe if I just go to sleep, I'll wake up and realize this was all a terrible dream.

Tues, March 17

I can't hide from it anymore. Wishing and waiting isn't going to change things, so I might as well face it.

Shawn says Ada is dead.

He told me he asked around, put the word out to everyone he knows that we were looking for her. Three separate people came and told him the same thing. Hard to argue with that. I asked him how it happened, but he just shrugged.

"These things happen," he said. "It could have been any of us. It was almost you, the night I found you."

"You think she was murdered?"

"Maybe. Maybe killed for some cash, maybe an OD, maybe went to sleep in a Dumpster one cold night and didn't wake up. It happens all the time."

"But the police—"

"What do the police care about one more dead hooker? Unless she has family that are looking for her . . ."

I shook my head sadly, remembering my encounter with Ada's mom. Not likely that she was aware enough to even wonder what had happened to Ada.

I don't know what to do with myself. In a weird way, I don't even know who I am anymore. Ada's been the only person who really mattered to me for so long. My best friend. My only real friend. My only true family. The only person who really cared for me. How do I go on without her?

Mon, March 23

I haven't updated here in a little while. I didn't know how to talk about what's been going on, or maybe I just didn't want to. But I might as well say it.

I've been sleeping with Shawn. At first I didn't know what to make of it. All I knew was that it was something I needed right then, but I wasn't sure where it was going or what it all meant. And when it started, my head and my heart were still so full of Ada, none of it even felt real. But now it's the only thing that does feel real. The only thing I can hang on to in this life that isn't pure misery.

You might think that after all the experiences I've had, sex would be the last place I'd look for comfort. But this is different somehow. It doesn't feel at all like the sex I've had with clients. It doesn't even feel like that first time with Damon. Not just bodies and parts and fluids. For the first time, I don't feel like an object for someone else to enjoy.

The first night I found out about Ada, I just needed someone. I needed to not feel so alone. And Shawn stayed with me, held me while I cried, listened to all my ravings. He made me feel safe.

But at the same time, I didn't understand it, so finally I asked him. I asked him why he was being so nice to me. Why did he take me home that first night? Why did he pay off my debt? Why did he take up my search for Ada, and why was he putting up with me right now? He's been sleeping on the couch for two weeks now just so I can have the bedroom to myself.

Shawn smiled shyly.

"I guess some of us have to balance out all the assholes of the world," he said. I didn't know what to say to that, so I just looked at him with tears in my eyes until he got shifty and awkward.

"Also . . . ," he said, hesitating, "there's kind of something else, too."

I nodded for him to go on. He took a breath.

"I like you," he said. "I like you a lot, and I have ever since the night I met you. And I guess I was just hoping that if I was nice to you, maybe . . . maybe you would start to like me too."

I had nothing to say to that, so I kissed him. And I told him he didn't need to sleep on the couch anymore.

Sat, March 28

How do you know when you're in love with someone? This seems like such a silly question to be asking right now, with all that's been going on in my life, and as usual I feel like a naive idiot not to know the answer. But I don't think I've ever felt it before. Back in my old life, I wanted Tyler so much, and it was a really huge crush, but I don't think I ever would have said that I loved him. I mean, I didn't even know him, really, and what I did know suggested that he was kind of a jerk. (Which turned out to be incredibly true.)

Sometimes I have warm feelings toward some of my clients, and I did like Damon a lot, but I don't know them, and I know they don't really care about me.

With Shawn it's so different from how it always has been. I know he cares about me. He shows me every day how much. I know we haven't been together long, but the past couple of weeks have been so intense. I can't say exactly that I'm happy. How could I be happy after what happened to Ada? But I feel loved and cared for, and I think I feel it back. I want to take care of Shawn the way he has taken care of me.

At least he's not sleeping on the couch anymore. But the truth is, I have taken too much from him. I could never repay him for all he's done for me, but I have to at least start contributing. Plus, I need to get out and do something. For a while, being tucked away in his bedroom was just what I needed. An escape from all the crap I'd been dealing with out there. A chance to catch my breath and sort out my thoughts. But now I've done that, and I'm starting to feel cooped up. I need to make myself useful.

Sun, March 29

Shawn's going to let me help out! It's actually funny how it worked out. He came in today with lunch, and I could tell he wasn't himself. He seemed upset and preoccupied, though he was clearly trying to hide it from me. But I made him tell me what was up. I'm not some fragile flower. He doesn't have to keep protecting me.

He didn't want to say anything at first, but eventually he admitted that he'd been distracted from real life by taking care of me for a while, and now he wasn't totally sure how he was going to make rent. But he told me not to worry about it, that he was resourceful and always figured out something.

So I explained to him that this worked out perfectly, because I'd just been thinking how I wanted to start pulling my weight around here. He doesn't need to keep me under glass. I can work. I can contribute.

He kind of laughed and asked what I could do to raise rent money. It's true that I really know only one way to make money, but what's wrong with that? I don't mind, if it will help.

Of course he was really against the idea at first. He said he didn't want me doing that kind of thing anymore. But I was like, "Come on! Who are you kidding?" I've done it before, and so has he. It should be no big deal to us.

Then I asked him if the idea made him jealous, and he admitted that it did. So I told him he was being silly. There's such a huge difference between what we do out there for money and what we do together for love. Out there is just a show, and this is for real. I told him I could never mix the two up. . . . Could he? And he said he couldn't either. So it's settled.

Tues, March 31

Last night was my first night back at work. It's different from working for Miss Irma, but not so much worse, I think.

How we worked it out is, I go out and stand in the park, visible but not too visible. When a car drives by going kind of slow, I step out and try to get his attention. If he stops, at that point Shawn comes over to check him out and make sure he knows I have someone looking out for me. And he handles the money, too, so I don't have to worry about that. If Shawn thinks the guy's okay, I either get in the car with him for a blow job, or we drive to a hotel. That costs more.

Last night there weren't any hotel dates, just blow jobs in cars. It really wasn't so bad. It's all over pretty quickly, and it's easy to stay detached. And I feel safer knowing Shawn is right there than I did going alone to those hotel rooms. The money isn't as good, but you can do so many more people in one night, so it almost evens out.

One thing we need to worry about is cops. That used to be less of an issue with Miss Irma. It could be a real nuisance if I get arrested, especially if they send me back to my parents.

I was wondering whether my parents would come look for me at any point, but Shawn told me not to worry too much about that. Odds are they went to the cops when I didn't come home, but given my recent history of erratic behavior, the cops will assume I'm a runaway, and they don't usually bother looking too hard for runaways, especially if they don't have any idea where you might be. But if the cops pick me up and they recognize me, they'll send me home immediately.

Shawn also has his own problems to deal with in the park, it turns out. I came back from a trick at some point to see some girl yelling at him and getting in his face. He managed to calm her down, though. I asked him about it and he told me not to worry about it, just an old girlfriend.

Oh, there's another kind of weird thing I learned tonight. Shawn talks differently when he's in the park compared to when he's home with me. The first time I heard him talking to the other guys who hang around the fountain, I almost laughed! He talks like a gangster or something, which is *so* different from how he sounds with me. And really different from how he sounded at Irma's party.

I asked him about it and he looked a little embarrassed, but he explained about playing roles again, and how we all need to be different characters in different situations. He had to play one character when he was appealing to male clients, but in order to get respect on the street, he has to act different. I asked him what role he's playing when he's with me, but he just smiled and said that with me he gets to be real, and that's why he loves me.

Thurs, April 2

Some girl came by the apartment just now looking for Shawn. He told me not to open the door for people who come by (his neighborhood is not the greatest), but this girl kept knocking and calling his name through the door. I thought it was probably the same girl he was arguing with the other night, but when I opened the door, it was someone different.

I told her Shawn wasn't there, and she was like, "I see that. Who the hell are you?"

So I told her I'm his girlfriend, and she started laughing. She said, "Yeah, I've heard that before. Has he got you working the streets yet?"

She left after that, but I can't stop thinking about what she said. She made it sound like Shawn is my pimp or something. But it's not like that. It's not like he has a whole stable of girls. Obviously I am the only one living here. And I'm not working for him. We're both working to pay the rent and support ourselves. Right? I don't know. I'll feel better after I talk to Shawn about it.

Thurs, April 2, later

Shawn and I just had our first fight. I asked him about the girl at the door when he came home. He told me it was another ex-girlfriend. I didn't say anything right away, but he could tell I wasn't totally happy, so he asked me what was up. I wasn't sure what to say, exactly, so I tried to keep quiet, but he kept pushing and saying I should tell him what's wrong, so finally I asked him: "Is she an ex-girlfriend or an employee?"

He didn't answer right away, so I pressed harder.

"And what am I?" I said. "Am I your girlfriend or your employee? Am I the talent?"

"Don't do this to me," he said. "Don't act like that. You know I love you. And working the park was your idea, remember? I didn't force you into anything. You volunteered."

"You're right, I did," I said. "But what about your other girls? Did they volunteer?"

Shawn looked hurt at this. "I don't force anyone to do anything," he said. "I'm not like that. It's not my style."

After that I shut myself in the bedroom with my journal to think for a while. I don't like how this looks or how it sounds. I don't want to believe it, but at the same time, I wonder how I could have been so stupid and naive. Of course Shawn is a pimp. Look at all the signs: his willingness to let me work the street, his insistence that he handle all the money, all the other girls he's always talking to at the park, plus his lowlife pimp friends. . . .

And he's right. I agreed to it. I walked away from Miss Irma and fell right into his business.

So what now? The thing is, I'm upset . . . but am I upset at Shawn? Or at myself for thinking our arrangement was something other than it was? I could leave him now, but where would I go? And why would I be leaving? Pride?

He never outright lied to me. He never said I was the only girl he was managing. I just assumed it. I knew I was hooking to earn money for him and that he was my protection when I worked. It just never occurred to me that that's basically what a pimp is.

But now that I've woken up, what does that change? Should I leave? I don't know what other options I have, except to go back to Miss Irma. Between Irma and Shawn, at least I trust Shawn more. At least now I know what my cut is, instead of it always being a mystery with Irma.

This isn't ideal, and it's not what I dreamed, but maybe it's what makes the most sense for me right now.

Fri, April 3

I sat down with Shawn and had a long talk about our situation.

I was angry at first, but more than that, I was concerned. All I could think about was what Miss Irma had said about competition. She made it pretty clear that she didn't look kindly on her employees turning around and setting up their own businesses.

But Shawn had that all figured out. He's being smart about it. He's not going after Irma's customers, and he's not using her talent. Except for me, but that's why he paid off my debt to Miss Irma. He says he went to her office and paid up the debt, and now they have an agreement, fair and square.

I wasn't sure how I felt about that. It sickened me a little to think Shawn bought me like a piece of meat. But he said it was a little late to get picky about that sort of thing. Fair point, I guess. He says he did what it took to get Miss Irma off my back, and that's what I wanted, wasn't it? It's no different from what I was trying to do for Ada.

I asked him why he was doing all this. Setting up his own business, I mean. Why not just stay with Miss Irma? But he turned eighteen this year, and just like Beth said, he noticed his client list drying up as Miss Irma stopped referring people to him. You don't get fired, he explained. You just get called less. And it gets harder and harder to support yourself, until you are driven to supplement your income by other means.

"Miss Irma likes to keep tight control over everyone in her stable," he said, "and once they become adults, she worries they'll start asking too many questions, become difficult to manipulate. So we're basically disposable to her."

Shawn was afraid of what would happen to him once he lost her backing, so he started watching her closely and taking notes.

"I want something bigger for myself," he said. "I don't want to be just another two-dollar rent boy. I want what Irma has, and I think I can make it happen, if I work hard." He took my hands in his. "If you help me," he said, "we can have it together. And when we run the show, we can treat people right and make it a decent business."

I do like that idea. And when he puts it that way, it makes sense. I always knew I didn't want to be selling my body for the rest of my life. That wasn't realistic. But without a high school degree, or college, or any real work experience, I didn't know how I was going to support myself. What Shawn's talking about, this is the first plan I've heard that makes long-term sense. Who knows how to run a business like this better than we do? Irma worked her way up from the bottom. We can do it too.

But right now we've got some cash-flow problems, which is why I have to hit the park again tonight.

Sun, April 5

I had a bad night tonight. When I finally got home and crawled into bed, Shawn started to paw at me and I just couldn't stand it. We had a bit of a fight, and I wound up asking him why he doesn't work the park. He just laughed at that, but I was serious.

"We could take turns," I pointed out. "Or we could make more money if we both did it."

He shook his head. "I have a different job now. There's better money in managing than working the streets."

"Long-term, sure," I said. "And that's what we'll both be doing soon. But just for now, wouldn't it be good to bring in some extra cash?"

Shawn got out of bed. "Trust me, it's not a good idea."

"I don't see why not."

"Because," he said, growing exasperated. "You can't do both. I can't let the people in this neighborhood know I ever turned tricks, all right? They won't respect me anymore. And in this game, respect is everything."

"But people respect Miss Irma," I said. "And everyone knows how she started out. And you're expecting me to—"

"It's not the same, okay? Can't you see how it's not the same?"

I didn't say anything.

"It's different for guys," he said quietly. "The people in the park, the people in this neighborhood, can't ever find out what I did for Miss Irma. Do you understand? People might call a girl bad names if she turns tricks, they might laugh at her, but if people knew that about me, if they thought I wasn't the person I seemed to be, it would be worse. Guys like me get hurt. Guys like me get killed."

I didn't know what to say to that.

"Do you understand?" he said. "It's important. In here we're the same. We've been through the same shit. But out there you can never talk about what I did. Do you get that?"

I nodded.

"It's like I said before. It's all about playing the role. And to make people believe it, you can't ever break character."

Mon, April 6

Another long night last night. Then, even when I fall asleep, it's like all I can dream about is climbing into and out of cars in the dark. I wake up more exhausted than when I went to bed.

It's a little too crazy to think that this is my life now. It's hard to believe that less than a month ago I was living at home and going to school like a normal teenager. I wonder what my old friends are doing now. Jenny and Eiko and John. Visiting college campuses, studying for the SAT? I wonder what they would think of who I am now, if they could even believe it. Would they recognize me like this? Would they ever talk to me again, if I went back?

Wed, April 8

I just realized I don't even know how many girls Shawn has working for him. Whenever we're both working the park, I try to circle around in his direction to check up on him from time to time, and he always seems to be talking to a different girl. I can't help wondering, did he recruit them all the same way he got me? Well, obviously not exactly the same way, but who knows? That guardian-angel bit does work pretty well. Maybe he saw them getting beat up by a pimp or a john and swooped in to save the day. Then they start dating, and before long, they're working. And it's on to save the next victim. Is Shawn more victimizer than savior?

No, it's not like that. Maybe it's not ideal, maybe it's not a perfect fairy tale, but at least Shawn treats his workers like human beings, unlike a lot of the pimps around here. He splits the take fairly, he keeps them safe, and he never gets violent or cruel.

And he loves me, right? I'm not like the other girls. He tells me that every day. But then . . . maybe that's what he told the girl who came before me. What if that were me? What if some new damsel in distress came along and I got downgraded from girlfriend to employee? What if that became my life, and I was just another girl working the park and handing my money over to Shawn, while he took a new girl home to his bed? Would I keep working for him?

I want to say that I would not. But where else would I go at this point?

Sat, April 11 (after midnight)

God, I've really done it now. Why couldn't I leave well enough alone? Sure, things weren't perfect, and maybe Shawn wasn't the hero I wanted him to be, but I was getting by. We were building a life. Then I had to go and ruin everything.

I'm crying so hard, it's hard to see what I'm writing, and the page keeps getting wet and smearing my ink. But I'm scared and

I have to quit my sniveling and stay quiet or else who knows what might happen. So I'm trying to write to calm myself down.

It started at the park, of course. I was supposed to be working, but as usual, I kept circling back to see what Shawn was up to. Lately I just can't stop thinking about the day some other girl wanders into the park with a problem and Shawn turns into Captain Save a Ho again. I tell myself if I can just keep an eye on him, I can stop that from happening, but I don't know how I think that will work. And in the meantime, every time he catches me, he gets pissed that I'm wasting time when I should be earning money.

Anyway, I saw him talking to this or that girl during the night, but it all seemed pretty normal until one time I noticed him with one of the usual girls, but they were arguing. And I knew I should just stay out of it and get back to work, but I couldn't help being curious, so I kept drifting closer, trying to hear what they were saying. It seemed like something to do with money, or respect, or both. He was being really verbally aggressive toward her, yelling and telling her not to test him. She kept sort of backing off, but then she would come back after a minute with a new comment, and he was calling her names, calling her a smart-ass, and the other guys joined in, encouraging Shawn and egging him on.

I knew I should stay away, but it really bothered me, the way he was treating her. I was anxious about him replacing me, but through it all, I had at least clung to the idea that Shawn wasn't so bad, as pimps went. He was a decent guy who didn't fit any of the usual stereotypes. But here he was, enacting them all.

All of a sudden, I was furious—at Shawn, and maybe even more at myself, for falling for his act. Shawn always said that what he did out here was an act and what he did back home was real, but the world doesn't work that way. He might think he was playing a role out here in the park, but none of this was make-believe. And I might have wanted to believe that what we had at home was real, but I was living a fantasy with Shawn just as much as with any other client I've been with.

I couldn't take it anymore. I knew I should wait until we were home alone to talk about it with him, but I wasn't thinking straight. I went right up and told him to leave that girl alone. The other guys in the park hooted and jeered at me, but I ignored them.

Shawn gave me a hard look. "Don't," he said simply, but I wanted an explanation.

"You told me you weren't like the others," I said, getting in his face. "You said you don't treat people that way."

"Don't do this right now," he said in a low voice. "We can talk about it later."

And the other guys started laughing again, but this time at

220

Shawn. Laughing about how he was letting a woman tell him what to do, I guess, but I wasn't paying much attention to them. I just wanted an answer out of him, and I wouldn't back down.

Then, the next thing I knew, there was a loud noise and I was reeling backward. It took a second or two before I even recognized the pain. Before I realized that he had smacked me. I stumbled back in a daze and somehow managed not to sink to the ground. After a few moments, I found my balance and stood up straight. Then, without a word, I turned and walked away from him, out of the park.

"Where do you think you're going?" he called after me.

"I don't know," I said, not turning around. "Away from you."

He jogged up and fell into stride beside me. "You can't take off by yourself. It's not safe," he said.

"Yeah? And I'm so safe here with you?"

"Fine," he said tightly. "Walk it off, if you have to. We can talk about this later."

After that he stopped following me and I just kept walking.

I went to the light-rail stop first, but at that hour it would be ages before one came by, and there were too many people around. Too many people who had watched what had happened and were eager to comment on it, offering advice or pity or criticism, or just wanting to stoke the drama for their own amusement. After a minute or two, I couldn't take it anymore

221

and started to just walk toward our apartment. I figured I could follow the rail line, and it would take me back to our neighborhood eventually.

But after a few blocks, I realized . . . Our neighborhood? Our apartment? That place wasn't mine. It was all his. The apartment was filled with his stuff, and the neighborhood was filled with his family and friends. Without Shawn I was totally isolated.

I was really starting to feel sorry for myself, all alone and friendless on the empty streets of Seattle in the middle of the night, and I was about to just find a doorstep to sit in so I could have a good wallow and cry while I tried to sort out the mess of my life. But then I became aware of a sound. Footsteps. And they were getting closer.

I tried to calm myself down and reassure myself that they had nothing to do with me. It was just another person out late at night, dealing with their own problems, minding their own business. But as I forced myself to focus, I realized I'd been hearing these footsteps for some time. *Click-clack, click-clack.* The sound had echoed through my thoughts for the past fifteen minutes without me even realizing it. I was definitely being followed.

I thought about turning around and confronting whoever it was, but I had nothing on me that could possibly be used as a weapon. I thought about breaking into a run and trying to make it home, but it seemed like a bad idea to let the stalker know where I lived. And I still haven't replaced my phone since that night I got jumped in the park, since every penny I've earned went to Shawn. So I couldn't even call the police.

Not knowing what else to do, I just kept walking, and the footsteps kept following, sometimes a little closer, sometimes a little farther away. At last I saw the opportunity I'd been hoping for: The footsteps had grown more distant, and up ahead of me was a narrow alleyway lined with garbage bins. I slipped in and sank down to sit on my heels behind one of the bins, desperately hoping to lose my stalker. I could make out the footsteps for a little while, but they stopped before they got too close. I heaved a sigh of relief, but I was still too scared to come out.

So that's where I am now. Scribbling in this journal to pass the time and make absolutely sure there is no one out there.

Shit. I just heard it again. *Click-clack*, *click-clack*. It's getting closer.

Sat, April 11, later

I hardly know what to say. Never in a million years did I think . . . I can't even figure out what to write! My thoughts are scattered all over the place. I need to focus. I need to write out what happened or else I will never believe it.

I remember that sound drawing closer, and I remember

closing my eyes and holding my breath. After that I'm not sure what happened. It was like a gray mist was swirling around me, and I think I must have passed out for a minute from fear. In any case, the next thing I remember is the feeling of an arm wrapped around me while something slid down my throat like liquid fire.

I sat up, sputtering, and scrambled around to see who was there. I nearly fainted again when I saw.

She was filthy, her long coat torn, her hair matted around her face and tucked into an inelegant bun, and there was a battered flask in her hand. But there was no doubt in my mind: It was Ada.

"I didn't mean to scare you," she said as I fought for breath. "But Shawn was right. It's a dangerous neighborhood. I couldn't let you walk it alone."

For a while I couldn't speak. My heart was still racing and my breath was short, but even more, I didn't know what to say. I had so many questions, I didn't know where to begin. I didn't know whether to be happy she was back, or furious that she had let me believe otherwise.

"You were dead," I finally gasped out after a couple more sips of the awful whiskey. "Shawn told me you were . . ."

Ada raised an eyebrow. "And what was it about Shawn that made you think you could trust what he said? I told you back at the party that he was trouble."

"But then why . . . ?"

"I had to disappear for a while," she explained. "You must have seen that. I tried to keep you out of the whole thing, when Miss Irma came sniffing around about the Damon business. I told her to leave you alone, but I knew she wouldn't listen, so I told you to stay away from her. You should have done what I said."

My eyes filled with tears. It was too much to process: the euphoria of having her back, along with the pain of having disappointed her.

"I was worried about you!" I said, choking back my emotion. "You didn't tell me where you'd gone. You just disappeared. Miss Irma was the only person who had any chance of telling me what happened to you."

"I couldn't tell you," said Ada. Her voice was calm and steady, but there was guilt in her expression. "It was too risky. If Irma got to you . . ." Ada put a hand to my cheek and looked into my eyes. "You don't know what she's capable of."

"I wouldn't have told her," I insisted. "I'd never have betrayed you."

"I know," said Ada. "But this was safer for us both." She grimaced a little. "Or it would have been, if you'd only stuck to the plan."

"The plan you never told me about!"

Ada dropped her gaze. "I'm sorry," she said. "I didn't know. . . . It never occurred to me. . . ."

225

"What?"

"I never imagined you'd come after me. That you would care enough to—"

"Of course I would. I always would."

She smiled weakly. "We shouldn't stick around here," she said. "Anything could happen. Can you take me back to Shawn's place? I could use a shower."

"What if he comes back?"

"I saw him go off drinking with his little pimp friends," she said. There was something slightly vicious in her tone. "He won't be back before morning."

As we walked the rest of the way home, Ada told me her story. Beth must have tipped off Miss Irma right after the Valentine's party, because that's when Irma went after Ada. Of course, Miss Irma always knew that Ada didn't have the cash, but she was willing to strike a deal. She told Ada they could settle up quicker if Ada took on dates with some of the more . . . demanding clients. The ones who like to make special requests.

Ada balked, but Miss Irma told her to grow up. She told her she wouldn't be sixteen forever, and at some point she was going to need something other than her youth to build her career on. Taking on kinkier clients would be a good career move. And if she did it, Irma promised not to try to get the money out of me.

It seemed reasonable enough, so she went along with it. But after a couple of dates, she couldn't do it anymore. I asked her what happened, but she wouldn't tell me. She just got a hard look in her eyes.

On top of that, Irma's goons keeping an eye on her made her mother's delusions get worse, until one day she wouldn't let Ada in the house. Ada decided her mother would be better off if she just skipped out, so she called an aunt to come by and look in on her, and Ada disappeared.

"Disappeared," I repeated. "What does that even mean? Did you go to another country or something?"

"I might as well have. I was in the Jungle."

"The Jungle? Like . . . South America?"

"Close enough. It's right here in the city. A patch of land between the freeways, too narrow and steep to develop. It's turned into a kind of no man's land, reclaimed by nature but not like a park, with paths and flower beds. It's wild, and so are the people who live there. You go there when you have nothing left to lose and nothing to live for. It's all junkies and crazies, and the people who are neither are even worse. They call it the Jungle, but they should just call it Hell."

"Jesus, Ada. How could you—"

"I didn't mean for you to think I was dead, but I needed to stay gone long enough for Miss Irma to stop looking for me, and I didn't know how long that would be. As it happens, I got lucky. Some poor slut died in a Dumpster, and a handful of people decided it was me. That was enough to convince Miss Irma, and Shawn too, as it turned out. And you."

"But that was a while ago! Why didn't you come back before?"

"News doesn't travel quickly to the Jungle. I didn't hear about my own death until a couple of days ago. At that point, I went to Jen, but Jen's gone. Beth was there, though, and she told me you'd been around looking for me."

"And before that, you never even tried to get in touch with me?" Even in my relief at having her back, I couldn't hide how hurt I was that she had forgotten me.

Ada stopped me and looked me in the eyes. "I thought you were at home with your parents. I wanted to tell you, but I thought you were safe, and I knew I would only mess that up. All I could think of was how much better off you'd be if you'd never met me. I wanted to give you a second chance at your real life."

I grabbed her by the arm. "Ada," I said, "you are my real life."

I think she finally believes me.

Sat, April 11, early morning

Ada's out of the shower now. She was starting to put back on her grubby clothes that she's been living in God knows how long, but I stopped her and gave her something of mine to wear. It's funny. It's almost like we're back to where we started, only this time she's wearing my clothes instead of me wearing hers. I still think she looks better in them, though, no matter whose they were to begin with. Even as skinny as she is right now.

"So what are we going to do?" I asked her as she studied her new look in the mirror.

She caught my eye in the reflection. "What are you ready to do?" she asked.

"Ready?"

Ada turned around to face me. "You and Shawn," she said. "Is that over now?" She dropped her eyes when I didn't answer right away. "I know how it is," she said. "I've seen it a million times. A girl gets smacked around a little; she gets angry, says she's going to leave. In the morning, she's making him breakfast and saying how sorry she is that she upset him."

"Ada, no," I said in horror. I reached out to take her hand. "No," I said firmly. "It's not like that. Even before tonight, I think a part of me already knew he was no good and was looking for a way out. I was just scared of being on my own."

Ada smiled. "But now you're not."

"Now I'm not. But maybe we should leave soon. It's getting light out, so he could be home any minute. And I'd rather not see him again."

229

Ada squeezed my hand tighter. "One more time," she said. "Can you deal with him one more time? If you disappear, he'll look for you. We need to see him once more, to make sure he'll leave you alone." I nodded and she dropped my hand. "Good," she said. "Besides, me and him have a little business to transact."

Sat, April 11, late morning

We're at Beth's now. She and Ada never liked each other, and she definitely wasn't my friend either, but when we had no place else to go, she was the one who took us in.

It probably helped that we gave her money.

That's part of what Ada wanted to stick around Shawn's place for, it turned out. While we waited, she started ransacking the apartment, going through all the drawers and closets. I asked her what she was looking for.

"His gun," she said.

"He doesn't have one," I told her.

"Are you sure?" she said. She turned and stepped into my space, looking deep into my eyes as if she could read the truth of my statement there. "Are you absolutely sure? Because this information could be very important in the conversation we're about to have. Life and death."

I nodded, to show I understood.

"But he doesn't have one," I said. "It was one of the things

230

he was saving up for, before I came around. There was one he wanted to buy. He was planning on it, but we didn't have the cash yet."

Ada nodded and relaxed a little. "Good," she said. "That will make this a little easier."

It wasn't much later that we heard his footsteps on the stairs. Ada motioned to me to be quiet, then silently moved behind the door just as we heard Shawn's key in the lock. He opened the door to see me sitting in his armchair and let out a sigh of relief.

"I'm glad you're here," he said. His words slurred a little, and I remembered Ada had said he was out drinking. But he was clearly trying to make up with me. "I'm sorry about last night," he went on. "You know I would never have done that, except—"

Ada slammed the door shut behind him.

Shawn jumped so high at the sound that I almost laughed. But that was nothing to how spooked he was when he turned around and saw Ada standing in front of him.

"Ada?" he said. "How in the hell? You—you're dead!"

"Not exactly," said Ada. "But you've done yourself a favor. You convinced me you really did think I was dead and you weren't lying before. That will make this go easier for you."

"What are you going to do?" he said. "Beat me up? I must have fifty pounds on you. And if you had a gun, you'd be pointing it right now."

"I don't have a gun," said Ada, "and neither do you. But you do have something that doesn't belong to you."

Shawn looked down at me, then back to Ada. "Take her," he said. "She's yours."

Ada made a disgusted face. "Really, Shawn? That's not what I meant. She's a person, not a thing, and you can't trade her back and forth. No. I want the money she earned that you never paid her."

Shawn hesitated, and even though I knew by now that he was a creep, it still hurt a little that he was more reluctant to give up the cash than me.

"How much did he pay you for all the streetwalking you've been doing?" Ada asked me.

"We were going to split it fifty-fifty."

"But how much did you actually see?"

"None yet. He was holding it for me."

"Not anymore," she said.

"You don't have a weapon," said Shawn. "Why should I do what you say?"

"I don't have a gun," agreed Ada, "but I do have a weapon. My weapon is your past. Give her what she's owed, or we'll go door-to-door in this neighborhood like a couple of Jehovah's Witnesses, telling everyone you know what you were doing when you were employed by Miss Irma. What do you think they'll say, Shawn, when I tell everyone what a good little cocksucker you used to be?"

Shawn didn't answer right away, but I could see panic in his eyes. It was gnawing at him, preventing him from thinking of any way out of the situation. After a minute, he walked over to a small safe under his desk and opened it. We watched him count out half the money, and Ada made him hand it to me.

"Thank you," I said.

"Don't thank him," said Ada. "All that is yours."

After that we went back to Beth's and more or less threw ourselves on her mercy. Thanks to Jen still being mixed up in the correctional system, Beth is behind on the rent and on the point of being evicted, so I think she was actually pretty happy to see us and our wad of cash. Too bad that took a big chunk out of it, but there will be time to worry about that tomorrow.

For now we're both exhausted from running around all night. There's only Jen's narrow bed to sleep in, so we'll have to share, but I don't mind. To be honest, now that I have her back, I just want to keep Ada as close as possible, so she doesn't slip away again.

Sun, April 12

I'm worried about Ada. We fell asleep yesterday morning curled up together in Jen's bed, and I felt the safest and happiest that I have felt in ages. Ada was alive! And for the first time, my dream of us living together and leaving a life of prostitution felt like it might be within my grasp.

We slept like that through the day, but come night I woke up to find myself struggling to kick the blankets off me. I was boiling hot even though the apartment was chilly. That's when I realized it was Ada. She was burning up and making us both sweaty and miserable. I got up and got a cool, wet washcloth for her face, then managed to fall back to sleep. But this morning she still feels hot, and she hasn't woken up yet, even though she's been asleep for almost twenty-four hours.

If she's sick, I guess the rest is good for her, so I'm not going to wake her up.

Mon, April 13

I went out and got some orange juice, chicken soup, and vitamins for Ada, using a bit of Shawn's money. My money, I should say. I earned it, and it's mine. I guess I still have a ways to go, breaking out of the mental habits I learned with him.

When I got back, Ada was awake! So that's good news. I

made her soup and she took a shower, and after a little while she even started to get a bit of her color back. She says it's just a cold she picked up while living on the streets. It's been pestering her off and on for a while, but now that she has a roof over her head and a warm bed to sleep in, she'll shake it off soon. She's so skinny, though! That can't be good for her health. I have to make sure she eats well while she's getting better, even though it means dipping into our little pot of money.

Speaking of which, I guess we need to start thinking about what comes next. This place is dingy and kind of a dump, but it's good enough for now, and I think Beth will let us keep staying here as long as we can help out with the rent. But the money I earned with Shawn isn't going to last long, with Seattle rents being what they are. I really, really don't want either of us to have to go back to hooking, so we're going to have to think of another solution.

Wed, April 15

Ada's feeling a bit better, so we had a talk about the future. She wants to stay here with me, which is a huge relief. To her too, I think. She still finds it really hard to believe I don't want to just go home to my parents, and I know she worries that as soon as things get difficult, I'll change my mind and go back, but I'm doing my best to reassure her that's not true. That I would never abandon her.

But that still doesn't solve the money problem. She mentioned that as soon as she was feeling a little better, she'd get in touch with Miss Irma. Now that her debt's been paid, she doesn't have to hide out from her anymore.

Ada shook her head and laughed in amazement when I told her I wanted us to support ourselves with legal jobs and quit hooking for good. But she said that she believed in me, and if anyone could figure how to make that work, it was me.

I just hope I'm worthy of the faith she's putting in me. God knows I don't really have any experience in this area. But I have to try. That life was no good for either of us. There has to be something better.

I guess tomorrow I'll start looking for HELP WANTED signs and pick up a few applications. And online postings too. Maybe there will be some stuff there—Beth said she'd let me borrow her laptop, and I picked up a cheap prepaid cell phone so people can contact me. I know the money won't be what we're used to, but normal people support themselves with normal jobs in this city, right? I can make this work.

Thurs, April 16

I picked up some applications today. I'm going to work on filling them out tomorrow. And while I was out, Ada found some stuff online that has a lot of potential. The details are vague, but it looks like you can make a lot of money, which would be good right now.

Ada says she's feeling better, but she still seems pretty listless to me, and she's running a fever again. I'm going to try to make her eat some more soup, then get to work on these applications.

Fri, April 17

I'm stressed out about these job applications. Beth explained to me that I'll be better off if I lie and say I'm over eighteen, because sixteen-year-olds are only allowed to work twenty hours a week in this state. The idea is that you're not supposed to work too much while you're in school, but I haven't seen the inside of a school in ages. So how does this law help me?

It's so frustrating. I'm just trying to make an honest living. To support myself legally, without any help from my parents. The whole idea of this was to work at something legitimate, so I wouldn't have to be looking over my shoulder all the time, worrying about cops. But how legitimate is my new life going to be if I have to lie to maintain it? I'm still going to be worried all the time about being found out.

But there's no way Ada and I will be able to survive on part-time pay.

Maybe I'll work on my applications for those online postings. Those don't seem to ask so many questions.

Mon, April 20

I feel really productive today! I turned in a whole bunch of applications, both in person and online. Something has to come through.

Wow. I had no idea how exhausting this whole process was. I feel like I should write more about what's going on, but right now all I want to do is curl up in bed with Ada and watch bad TV. She's been sleeping all day, so hopefully that means her fever is down. All this will be easier when she's feeling better and we both have jobs. Then everything won't feel so desperate. We just have to hold on until then.

Fri, April 24

Ada's worrying me again. I ask her every day how she's feeling, and every time she smiles brightly and says, "Better!" But not fine, or good, or all better. Honestly, I'm not sure I believe her. I don't know if it's wishful thinking on her part, or if she's lying to protect me. All I know is that two weeks is a long time for anyone to be sick with a cold or the flu without any real improvement.

I haven't heard back about any of my applications yet, so I sent out a few more.

Fri, April 24, later

I got responses from one of the online applications! It says I can start right away. It sounds perfect. The money's pretty good, the work looks easy, and I can do it from home, so I can keep an eye on Ada.

The only problem is there are start-up costs. Basically, you have to wire them some money to pay for the materials you need before you can get started. Kind of like how I had to pay for my phone and stuff when I started with Miss Irma. It sucks because it's basically going to eat up the last of what we had saved, but you know what they say: You have to spend money to make money.

Wed, April 29

I haven't heard back from that online place since I wired them the cash. I've sent them a bunch of messages. Rent is due at the end of the week, and I don't have it. I know what we're going to do if they don't come through soon. I might have to turn some tricks to make ends meet, even though I really didn't want to fall back on that.

Ada offered to, but with how she looks right now, I'm honestly not sure anyone would take her up on it. At least she still has contact info for some of her old clients. Miss Irma wouldn't like us setting up dates behind her back, but it's a possibility.

Fri, May 1

Today was not good. Ada fainted in the shower, and I finally convinced her to let me take her to the hospital. I've been trying all week, but she always said it was just a cold, she just needed some rest, and I wanted to believe she was right. But a part of me has known for a while now that she's really not well, and we need to do something about it. I'm just so scared. I lost her once already.

No point in thinking about that. They admitted her to the hospital and said it looks like pneumonia. They said it had gotten pretty bad, but they also said that it would probably get better now that she's being treated.

I stayed there with her for a couple of hours, but eventually the nurses sent me home and told me to let her rest. Then Beth started nagging me about rent, so I did what I had to do. Called up a couple of the numbers Ada had written out, made some appointments. I had one this evening. I'll do another tomorrow, and that should see us through for a little while.

Mon, May 4

I got a job! A real, legal job.

I got a call this morning from one of the fast-food places where I applied. I went in for an interview, and they hired me on the spot! I'm so excited. I feel like things are finally coming together. Maybe I can even help Ada get a job there too, in a little while.

The job is basically working the cash register all day, plus mopping the floors and cleaning the bathrooms during the off-peak hours. Doesn't sound great, but it's better than nothing. I start tomorrow!

Tues, May 5

First day of work was okay. Too exhausted to write much more. Didn't even get a chance to visit Ada today, but I will make it to the hospital tomorrow. Hopefully, they will release her soon and I won't have to trek over there anymore.

Wed, May 6

I went to the hospital right after work today, hoping that this would be the day they released Ada and let her come home. When they let me in to see her, she really did look a lot better. Not so thin and gaunt anymore and with a lot more energy. But her expression was sad and serious, even when I tried to cheer her up with funny stories from work and stuff.

After a while she stopped me and said she had to tell me something. Then she told me not to freak out, which is never a good start to a conversation. I told her to just come out with it.

Ada has AIDS. Or HIV. I don't know. It's not totally clear right now. Ada was calm enough, but she didn't seem to have absorbed all the details. I guess I can't really blame her. It's hard enough just to wrap your head around something like that.

I had promised her I wouldn't freak out, but I couldn't help it. I started crying. Ada held my hand for a little while, but when I didn't stop, she scooted over a bit and let me climb into the hospital bed with her. She held me and stroked my hair as if I were the one dying, not her.

But I'm not supposed to say stuff like that. Once I had calmed down a bit, Ada whispered reassuring things to me about how it's not a death sentence anymore, and now that they know why she was so sick, they can treat it and she'll be healthy enough to come home soon. She'll have to take a lot of pills and be extra careful about certain things, but it's not like she's going to die tomorrow.

I know that, but still, it's not like it's going to be easy. This changes things. Realistically, we need to think about what this means for us, and our life.

I can't think about that stuff now, though. I just need to let it sink in. And I need to get to sleep. I have to be at work early tomorrow morning.

Fri, May 8

I asked Ada today how it happened. How she got sick. When I first found out, I was too shocked to even think about how she got infected, and after that I wondered, but I felt awkward about asking. But finally my need to know won out over my awkwardness.

Ada just sort of shrugged it off, though. She called it a "little souvenir" of her time in the Jungle. I don't understand, because she knows better. She always made me swear to use condoms with clients every time, no matter how much they tried to pressure me, but she just said that once you're living on the street, priorities change.

That's when I got angry with her, which I know isn't fair, but I couldn't help it. How could she let this happen to herself? How could she do it to me? That's selfish of me, I know, but it hurts.

After that she didn't want to talk about it anymore, and I felt like a jerk. I get the feeling that stuff happened when she was living out there. Stuff she can't talk about, even to me. Part of me wants to know everything, but another part of me thinks she's right. I don't know if I could handle hearing about it.

Some friend I am.

Fri, May 15

I haven't written in a while. To be honest, there hasn't been a whole lot to say. My days are split between work and visiting Ada in the hospital, and when I come home at night, I'm so exhausted that I can barely manage to microwave a frozen burrito before falling into bed. At least Ada is looking better these days.

But work is . . . I don't know. I keep telling myself that this is better than hooking, that this is a better life. And it is. It's safer. I'm not going to get beat up or infected with a disease or forced to take a dangerous drug. That's important. But in other ways . . . It sounds crazy to say, but sometimes this life doesn't feel so different.

I thought it would be less dehumanizing at least, but in a way it's even worse. All day long, for hours and hours, I'm doing the same actions, going through the same motions, until I feel like a machine. People say prostitution is "selling your body," but what am I selling at this job? Definitely not my mind. They just need someone to stand there, to work the cash register, to push the mop around. Any warm body could do it. But instead of doing an hour of work a day, I'm stuck there for eight or more. And I get paid half as much.

At least hooking was good training for this position. All that time I spent figuring out what clients wanted, smiling when I was miserable or in pain, making people believe I was enjoying myself, those are all pretty useful skills in the new job too. That whole idea of giving people their fantasy—I'm still doing it. Only instead of pretending to be a Japanese schoolgirl, I'm pretending to be a normal teenager who loves her job and is happy to serve them. Which is almost as much of a lie.

Oh, and I got my first paycheck and got to see how much was taken out for taxes and stuff. Not sure how this is different from when Irma and Shawn took their cuts from everything I earned.

Tues, May 26

I got fired today. They moved my shift around so I had to visit Ada in the morning before work, and then I wound up coming in late too many times. I know it's my fault. I'm such an idiot. But the time I spend with her is the only time I'm happy all day. It's so hard to make myself leave to go to that dark hole-in-the-wall that reeks of rancid meat. Well, I guess now I don't have to anymore.

I don't know what we're going to do for money, though. Even when I was working, it really wasn't enough to live on, so it's not like I had anything saved up. And it's going to take me a while to find something else.

I might try panhandling for a while. I hear sometimes people make okay money doing that.

Thurs, May 28

Beth is kicking me out. I can't say I blame her. I'm pretty useless as roommates go. Not only am I broke, but I'm also miserable all the time, so I'm not exactly good company.

She found someone else who wants to move in right away.

A new girl who just started working for Miss Irma. I met her tonight, which was awkward, but she seems nice enough. She's a little like me, actually. She grew up in a nice suburb, unlike most of the people who work for Miss Irma. But she says her father started raping her when she turned thirteen, and that's why she ran away. Jeez. Maybe she deserves this apartment more than I do.

Beth was surprisingly not a complete jerk about it when she told me. She just sat me down and said I had better find another situation, because this girl would be moving in tomorrow. And when I started to cry, she said maybe I should go back to my parents . . . which only made me cry more.

I don't know. Maybe she's right. It's true I'm not like the rest of them. My parents are tough, but they aren't abusive, and I know they love me and would take me back. But I also know that's not all they would do. After this, after all I've put them through—running away, stealing money, being completely out of contact for so long, to say nothing of how I treated them before I left—there's no question that the minute I came back they would book me on the next flight to Taiwan. And I understand it's not punishment. I know that when they made that threat, it was out of concern, not cruelty. They think they need to get me away all from all the bad influences that got me to this place. And how can I blame them? I see how it must look from their perspective.

But that's not the whole story. They would never understand about me and Ada. They can't possibly understand that none of this was her fault and she always did everything she could to protect me.

And they'll never understand that I promised I would stick with her and that I wouldn't give up and go home, no matter how bad things got. And with the way she is now, there's just no way I can abandon her, completely on her own, without a friend in the world. I know very well that going home means getting sent away, and that means leaving Ada. I can't do it.

So I'll figure something out. I have to. Even if it means living on the streets for a while. If Ada did it, I can too. And if it means turning tricks again, at least until I can get back on my feet, I can handle that. I did it before, and it didn't kill me. I'll do whatever I have to.

Wed, June 3

Why is it always raining in this damn city? I really don't want to sleep in a stinky old Dumpster, but I am so sick of being soaked all the time. At this point I'd be willing to blow someone just for a sandwich and a couple of hours in a bed. I bet Miss Irma would laugh at that, after the money I used to make with her, but it's hard to attract much attention from johns when you look like a drowned rat. And I don't even want to think about what I smell like.

In a few hours I can go visit Ada in the hospital. At least it's dry there, and I might be able to snag some food off her tray. Stealing food from AIDS patients! That's definitely a new low in my life.

Tues, June 9

I got caught sleeping in Ada's bed with her. It's not the first time I've been caught, but the nurses and orderlies always looked the other way before. They even let me stay past visiting hours a couple times. I think they probably had figured out that I didn't have anyplace else to go. Sometimes an hour or so snuggled up with Ada is the only real sleep I get all day.

But this time a nurse woke me up and made me leave the room. He stood out in the hall with me and explained about how sick Ada is. Yes, she is looking much better now, but she still has a severely compromised immune system, and any random bug I have could easily get passed to her. He was being really nice and gentle about it, but I got the message. All you have to do is look at me these days to see that I am probably crudded up with all kinds of diseases. Starving and sleeping in the rain and fucking random people for pocket change (even if I do always use a condom) is not exactly a healthy lifestyle.

I tried to just nod and show I understood, and I know he wasn't trying to be hurtful, but I couldn't help tearing up. I just felt so awful and guilty, thinking I could be the reason Ada gets sick again. I'm supposed to be visiting to make her feel better, but I've been so selfish lately, using my time in the hospital with her as a little vacation from my own wretched life.

So after that conversation, I basically just wanted to find a Dumpster to crawl into and die and not be a bother to anyone anymore, but the nurse wouldn't let me go. Instead, he took me to an office and had me sit down, and he brought me some food. After a while a woman came to talk to me. She said she was a social worker, and immediately I panicked that she was going to turn me over to my parents or the cops or get me put into foster care or something. I've heard enough stories not to want that.

But she calmed me down and said she wasn't going to make me do anything. She just wanted to talk and maybe see if she could help me. And she said I could leave if I wanted to, but she hoped I would stay and talk awhile. I almost walked out right then, because I didn't think anything good could come of this, but I could see out the window that it was still raining, and I just couldn't face going back out into that yet. Another hour in a warm, dry place didn't sound so bad.

So she asked me about my parents, and I told her I couldn't go back there. And I could see that she was thinking they beat me or raped me or whatever, like so many of the other kids I've run into, and I felt bad letting her think that, so I wound up explaining the whole situation. About how they would send me away and then I would never see Ada again, and there isn't anyone else to take care of her (even if I'm not doing a very good job of taking care of her right now). She listened to my whole story and she didn't say I was wrong or stupid or anything.

After I was done, she sat and thought for a while, and then she asked me if she could call my parents. And I said absolutely not. The less they know about where I am or how I'm doing, the better. Then she said, "What if I can get them to agree not to send you away? What if I explain to them that you'll go back home with them, but only on the condition that you get to stay in Seattle and you can visit Ada here in the hospital every day?"

I didn't say yes right away. I was still really sure that my parents would freak out and take me away from her, no matter what this lady thought. But I stuck around and we talked about it for a while. It was almost like a negotiation, where she was trying to get me to agree to certain conditions in exchange for certain promises. I wound up agreeing that if my parents would let me see Ada every day, I would go home and start going back to school and do whatever I had to do to catch up in my classes. And I would promise never to run away again and not do any drugs or alcohol (which had never been a temptation for me anyway, but she wanted me to promise), and not contact anyone else who had anything to do with my life as a prostitute—Miss Irma or Shawn or any of the other talent or clients.

Honestly, that all sounded fine to me. I don't want anything to do with that world anymore. I won't mind going back to regular life and living with my parents and everything, as long as I can stay in touch with Ada and be there for her through her recovery. In all of this, Ada was all I really cared about.

So I wound up agreeing to everything the social worker was saying. And then she asked if she could call my parents right then and put me on the phone with them, but I wasn't ready to do that yet. I was scared that if I spoke to them, they would start telling me what to do and how it was going to be and I wouldn't know how to say no or stand up for myself. Or they would make promises but they might not keep them.

She said she understood, so we agreed that she's going to call them tomorrow and try to talk to them, but she won't give them any information about where I am or how to find me. She'll just tell them that I'm okay. I guess I would at least like them to know that.

And then, if they want me to come home, she'll explain about our agreement and we'll take it from there.

Wed, June 10

I spoke to the social worker (Jane) again today after visiting with Ada. She said she left a message with my parents, and they called back! And they were really, really happy to hear I was okay. That's nice to know, I guess. I think I was a bit worried that they would just be angry and disappointed and maybe not even want me back. But Jane said they had been really worried and they just want to talk to me.

She said she told them a bit about our agreement, and they're going to come meet with her later today to talk about it in person. She asked me if I wanted to be there, but I think it's better if I'm not. I just think that we would all get really emotional, and I'm not sure I'd make the best decisions with them right there in the room with me. I'd rather they agree to the terms we set out before I see them.

Thurs, June 11

Jane met with my parents yesterday and she says they agreed to our terms! She didn't want to go forward with anything without talking to me first, but she says if I'm okay with it, she'll arrange a meeting and I can go home with them. I think I'm going to do it!

I talked to Ada about it today too. I hadn't told her anything about Jane or my parents before, because I didn't want her to worry that I was thinking about leaving her. And I know how she is. She would always try to talk me into whatever she thought was best for me and not give a thought to herself. So I wanted to make this decision on my own, without letting her or anyone else influence me too much.

But I told her today that I was thinking about it, and she said she was really happy for me and that I should do it. And I explained about how I would still come see her every day, so she wouldn't even notice a difference really. And then she made a joke about how she hoped I would at least smell better. But her eyes were wet when she said it, and I started bawling, of course, and then the nurse made me leave again because he said I was getting Ada overexcited. But he let me back in after a few minutes.

I'm going now to tell Jane that I want to do it. I have to admit, I'll be glad to see my mom again. And to sleep in my own bed!

Wed, June 24

I haven't written in a while. At first I was just going through too much stuff to even think about this journal, and then, well, to be honest, things were going so well, I was afraid that putting it into words might jinx it all. Silly, I know.

But things are going well. Better than I had any right to expect, really. Ada's still in the hospital, but she is *so* much better, and starting to really get her strength back. The doctors say they'll probably release her at the end of the week. After that, it looks like she's going to move back in with her mom. I was nervous about this, but her mom's finally gotten on medication, so that should change things. She's even been to visit Ada a few times, and Ada says she is so much better. Plus, Ada's aunt helped her mom get signed up for Social Security disability insurance, which should help them out a lot. With that money coming in, they won't be dependent on Ada to support them.

As for me, I've been adjusting. My parents have been pretty great, all things considered. They were really happy to have me back, and they've been okay with me going to visit Ada regularly, even though I know they don't approve of her. My brother, Mark, came back from college for a while too, and that helped smooth things over. He told my parents that he is dropping his engineering major and switching to theater arts! That was a huge surprise to all of us and not a particularly happy one for my parents.

Mark took me out for milk shakes the other day and we talked about it. It seemed really out of the blue, but he said he'd actually switched over to mostly theater courses some time ago; he just hadn't felt brave enough to let our parents know. But when he found out everything that was going on with me, he decided to come home for a little while and tell them. He didn't say it in so many words, but I think he was trying to distract them. Maybe take a little of the heat off me. That was pretty cool of him.

I'm not sure if it worked, but we have all been getting along better lately, and I think Mom is coming around to the idea that she has to let us choose our own paths. In any case, there haven't been any more threats about getting sent to Taiwan, so at least they are holding up that end of the bargain.

I haven't gone back to school yet. The school year is practically over, and if I went back now I'd only flunk all my finals. Believe it or not, my parents actually suggested I take the rest of the semester off to just recover and get readjusted to living at home. Over the summer they're going to get me a tutor to help me catch up with everything I missed this spring.

It's weird. I always used to think of studying as a chore, but the truth is I'm kind of looking forward to learning stuff again. In any case, I don't find myself fantasizing about moving out on my own like I used to. I think living on the streets for a while cured me of my yearning for independence, at least for now.

I am nervous about going back to school in the fall, though. I have no idea what people have heard about why I disappeared for a while, or if anyone even noticed. I don't know what Tyler told people about me.

I wish Ada could come back to school with me, but everyone agreed that with her current health situation, she needs to be extra careful: Any random cold virus sweeping through the school could set her back. Once she's doing better, Jane found her a special program at one of the city schools, where they have more resources to deal with cases like hers. Which is great! But it leaves me on my own.

It's okay, though. It'll be weird for a few days, but I just need to be brave and work through it. I'm sure everything will get back to normal after that.

Editor's Note

This journal was found in the author's room shortly after her disappearance.

According to her parents, the author returned to classes in the fall. A few weeks into the semester, she went to school in the morning and never came home. A thorough investigation did not turn up any evidence at first. Police located her body two weeks later under a bush in the Beacon Hill area of Seattle between Interstate 5 and Interstate 90, referred to in this journal as the Jungle. Her body was mostly nude, covered in bruises, and forensic reports indicate the cause of death to be asphyxiation due to strangulation.

Witnesses recalled seeing her the previous week with a variety of different men, none of whom could be positively identified.

She was a good girl,

living a good life. One night, one party,
changed everything.

IN THE TRADITION OF *GO ASK ALICE*

Lucy in the Sky

Anonymous

One party. One taste.
No turning back.

**Read her story in her own words,
in the diary she left behind.**

She was an athlete

with a bright future. She only wanted
to lose a few pounds.

IN THE TRADITION OF *GO ASK ALICE*

Letting Ana Go

Anonymous

Once she started,
she couldn't stop. . .

Read her devastating journey in her own words,
in the diary she left behind.

SimonTeen

Simon & Schuster's **Simon Teen**
e-newsletter delivers current updates on
the hottest titles, exciting sweepstakes, and
exclusive content from your favorite authors.

Visit **TEEN.SimonandSchuster.com** to
sign up, post your thoughts, and find out what
every avid reader is talking about!